'There is an ancient  what might have bee of the biblical story understanding and app

Bible stories is known as Midrash, and Jacob the Son is an outstanding contemporary example of it. Roger Harper masterfully helps readers get on the inside of what biblical characters were thinking, feeling, and experiencing, and in so doing, he helps readers to not merely read the biblical story, but to experience its transforming power!'

Greg Boyd
Founder and Leader of Woodland Hills Church, Minnesota, Professor of Theology and Author.

Fresh View Books

Make you Think Books

Heaven and Earth Books

Jacob
the Son

Roger Harper

Roger is a UK Prison Chaplain and Contributor to
Premier Christianity Magazine

Ladder Media Limited
a Christian Equitable Company
www.laddermedia.co.uk

First published in Great Britain by Ladder Media 2022

This paperback edition
1

Cover design by Beatroot Media, © Ladder Media Ltd. 2022

A catalogue record of this book is available from the British Library
ISBN: 978-0-9561848-4-9

Printed and bound in Great Britain by Biddles, Kings Lynn

To Rebecca and Deborah,

my Best Women.

Thanks to

Tracy Chevalier who has helped shape this book and made it more detailed

Anne and Miriam and Jeremy for their improvements and encouragement

Rob and Alan who have stuck with Ladder Media through thin and thinner

Sharon, my beloved, whose enthusiasm for this book and for me has given confidence and delight and a fresh foundation of love

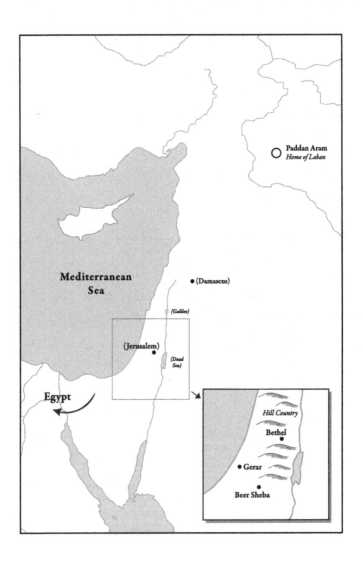

Genesis covers events which happened many years before they were written down. People who try to date the time of Jacob reckon this was between 1800 BC and 1600 BC

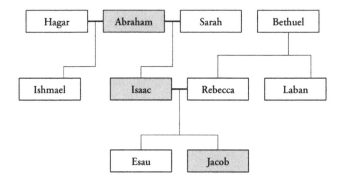

"Jacob is a morally ambivalent character—especially at the beginning of the story. He isn't the sort of person that you would pick out—especially if you were a hack writer—as the hero of the story. He does a lot of things that are pretty reprehensible, and it takes him an awful lot of time to learn better. And yet, he's the person who's put forward as the father of the 12 tribes of Israel. It's from this flawed person that the people emerges whose story, you might say, constitutes the fundamental underpinning of our culture. So you might think of that as a relief, too, because you're no knight in shining armour, with a pure moral past."

Jordan Peterson, former Canadian Professor of Psychology, author and prominent internet teacher, https://www.jordanbpeterson.com/podcast/s3-e13-biblical-series-jacobs-ladder/

Introduction

Many people know that Jacob dreamed of a ladder to heaven. Most do not know the message of that dream and whether Jacob heeded it. Many people know that Jacob cheated his twin brother, Esau, out of his blessing. Most do not know whether or how they were ever reconciled. Many people know that Jacob wrestled with God. Most do not know why God was determined to pin Jacob to the ground. Many people know that Jacob had his name changed to Israel. Most do not know how Jacob connived in the first genocide. Many people know that Jacob gave his son Joseph an amazing coat. Most do not know how Jacob angered Joseph in blessing his sons. Many people know that Jacob was promised blessing in the land we know as Israel / Palestine. Most do not know how he came to die an alien in Egypt.

As well as recounting and explaining the lesser-known times in Jacob's life, the three parts of *Jacob The Full Story* portray his thoughts and feelings, his conversations with others, and the background to the Bible account. Jews have long filled out their Bible stories in a tradition called midrash. Myjewishlearning.com explains: 'Midrash is commonly defined as the process of interpretation by which the rabbis filled in "gaps" found in the Torah. It is a literature that seeks to ask the questions that lie on the tips of our tongues, and to answer them even before we have posed them.'

Jacob The Full Story carries on and extends the Jewish midrash tradition in a fresh way. Some of the filling out comes from drawing on other parts of the Bible story, for instance the impact of Jacob's twin brother Esau choosing to marry two foreign wives compared to their father Isaac holding steadfastly to one wife, recounted earlier in Genesis. What would Jacob, and others, have thought about this double marriage? Imagination supplies the answers, creating dialogues of different points of view.

One filling-in, which you will read, is that, when Jacob had to leave his parents' home, he took servants with him. Jacob's father, Isaac, is called a very wealthy man. Would his son travel entirely on his own? Jacob's companions each provide a fresh, prophetic, perspective on his journey.

The words of the companions help to explain the story. Genesis is a 'show, don't tell' book. Genesis shows blessing coming to Jacob after he received the promise of blessing. The writer does not also specifically tell us that each blessing was the fulfilment of the promise. Genesis shows blessing being withdrawn from Jacob. The writer indicates reasons for the withdrawal of blessing within the story, but does not specifically tell us these reasons. In *Jacob The Full Story* Jacob's companions comment on the story from within the story. There is more telling as well as more showing, the telling expressing different points of view.

Among the voices we hear more than in Genesis is that of Rebecca, Jacob's mother. She is one of the great Jewish matriarchs, founding mothers. A long-standing Jewish tradition sees all the matriarchs as prophets, people who could hear God speaking and pass on what they heard to the people. At the beginning of Jacob's life, before he was born, Genesis tells us that Rebecca was able to go to God, question him, and hear an answer. *Jacob – The Full Story* brings out more of Rebecca's prophetic wisdom.

One question has been how to refer to the God of Jacob. Genesis mostly writes God's name as YHWH, unpronounceable letters which have long been replaced with the euphemism 'The LORD.' (Like saying 'Her Majesty' rather than the Queen's name.) But we are also told that this 'name' was first given to Moses, generations after Jacob. 'The LORD' is also now a characteristically Christian rendering of YWYH. Many Jews use 'Ha Shem' 'The Name.' The modern French Bible uses 'L'Eternel' 'The Eternal One.' I have chosen to focus on the distinctive belief in a single God held by Abraham's family, including his grandson, Jacob. Instead of 'the LORD' or 'Ha Shem,' you will read 'The One.' In a world where people believed in many gods, each behind one of the many powers in nature, Jacob and his family dared to believe that behind the manifold, sometimes competing, powers of nature, was One God.

In the Bible this God is known as 'the God of Jacob', more than 'the God of Abraham,' much more than 'the God of Moses.' This God has chosen to make himself known through the life of this man. Jacob had his name changed to Israel. 'The God of Israel' is the God of the same man.

As Jacob and Israel are the same person, how much is the story of the nation Israel the story of the man Jacob? Is the life of Jacob echoed in the life of ancient Israel, in the life of modern Israel? Read *Jacob - The Full Story* and decide for yourself.

The God of Jacob is the God of Christians as well as Jews. How are people of all cultures to relate to Him? *The Full Story* shines light on these questions for all people.

Chapter One

Two Boys

(Genesis 25:19-34)

'Yes, yes, yes! How many times does my son need to hear? Is there something wrong with your ears, already? You don't have a grey hair on your head and you're having memory problems?' Rebecca turned to Jacob from kneading the dough and smiled. She brushed back her hair, leaving white flour streaks above her right eye and onto her blue scarf. Upright sinuous. alert. Her large eyes, crowned with elegant eyebrows, settled on Jacob, no longer darting around. No wonder the singers called her a gazelle.

Jacob enjoyed the smile, the banter. 'Mum you look so good and you tell the story so well. Please!'

'My son needs stories, memories. Well, you can't eat them,' Rebecca beamed at Jacob, 'but if that's what you need, who am I to disagree?'

She attacked the dough, her muscles bulging. 'You have no idea! No idea of the thumping in my belly, the swishing

17

sick feeling that made me stumble, the weight. No rest, no sleep. But I would do it all again tomorrow to have my boys. How can you be so different when you were made at the same time in the same body?

'I knew there were two of you, at least! Or a monster with seven arms and ten legs. Oh, the bruising! And God, bless him, told me there were two. That helped. No accident! But even The One won't ever have to go through what I went through. The old women weren't so sure. "This is your first pregnancy, young lady. We've all had a difficult time, you know." Hah! I would have liked to see them carry such a battle inside them.

'When the pains came, it was a relief. The end drawing nigh. Oh God did I want you out in the world! Breathe, scream, scream, breathe. It's only women that can possibly do this kind of labour. You so much want your body to open up, but it's never done that before and you never thought it would feel like you had to be split so far and you want it and you think it's impossible and you can't carry on. Can we just have a day's rest in the middle? That would be good, God! But oh no, no rest from this labour. You have to do it. Breathe, scream, scream, breathe. It's only afterwards that your throat feels raw.

'At last, the promised words. "It's got a good hairy head." "It can't be long now!" "Push!" they say, four voices at once. That should be so easy! Well, you push, yourselves, as you've all done it before! Don't you know how drained I am?

'From somewhere came the urge to push.' Rebecca squeezed a large lump of dough and exhaled deeply, an animal straining, almost manly. "'It's a big one!" "Must be a boy, Rebecca!" "Push, just push, he's nearly there." Didn't they know how hard I was pushing? But he didn't seem to go further. He was squirming, he wanted to be in the great outdoors. You know when you grab a sheep between your legs to shear it? Just try to imagine that inside you, butting away at your bones. Oh my goodness! They talked of going to fetch the puller. You know, the wooden pincer things they use on the ewes. They tried to whisper but I knew. Where are you, God, when I need you? What have I ever done to deserve this? Treat me like a stupid sheep? If only my mother was here, she'd have known what to do.

'Another push came, with a belly war cry.' Rebecca made a sound like a roar and a groan and a shout of defiance to all the universe. Jacob's head recoiled, startled. 'You think that's loud? You should have heard the real thing. All the children in the camp went running to their mothers, believe me. They wouldn't come near me for weeks.

'It did the trick, it cracked the nut, it got the monster out. He surged forward with my war cry ringing in his ears. "Ooh! Hairy shoulders." "His skin's red." "No, it's not the blood, it's the skin." "Hairy chest." "We don't have to look to see if this one's a boy." The women's words were tumbling over themselves.

'I could relax a moment, maybe a few minutes, before the next one came. But no. Another body was there already. This one seemed to fit. Snug and gentle, even soothing, as it came out. Like a ripe banana. Or a baked loaf coming clean out of a tin.' Rebecca made a sound of a deep satisfied trembling, a long vibrating exhalation of ease and pleasure.

'And there you were, holding your brother's heel, while I just purred. No wonder I hardly had to do anything. You turned him into the puller. Clever man.' Rebecca smiled at Jacob.

'Esau screamed short and loud. He looked around him. He shook his leg and you let go. Esau lay still, looking up, waiting and ready for whatever came to him. You squirmed, you rubbed your face, you whimpered. You were so cute!

'You both needed me. Esau fed with great sucks, intent on the intake, no muscle moving. One breast was never enough for him. He drank deeply and swiftly and soon had no more need of me for two or three hours. You fed eagerly too, but shifted around and kept losing me. Then you nuzzled around and, with some help, you had another sip. Sometimes you let go and just looked at me. Your big blinking eyes finding mine. Your half a breast lasted twice as long as Esau's breast and a half. But it was a sweet time, a together time.

'The naming was simple because I decided to keep my mouth shut. Yes, before you say anything, I can do it. Ideally, I would have liked to give you what God had said you were, the ruler over your older brother. But I knew no-one else would understand. So it was simple, you named yourselves. Esau – Hairy. Jacob – Heel. I didn't mind your name not being too complimentary, at least not in your father's eyes. It has a hidden meaning. You're not really the heel, the low-lying cheat. You're the heel-taker, the grasper of strength outside yourself. That's who you are, Jacob. You'll go far.'

'I don't think I want to go far, thank you,' thought Jacob. 'Life here is fine for me.'

Jacob stomped about the store tent muttering loudly, 'O God! Where are you? Where?' He kicked at the sacks of barley and flopped down on the sloping side of heaped hay.

Jacob was feeling sore and insignificant. His twin brother Esau had made a joke about his weedy arms and their father had laughed instead of telling Esau off. He might as well not be there, for all his father noticed.

'So where on earth are you God? Miles away as usual?' The dry sweet grassy smell was one of his favourites. It took the edge off his annoyance. He also felt enveloped by the canopy of brown linen, which rested on poles of light wood. Piles of plump sacks reassured him, as everyone, with their plenty: hard beans, soft flour, fragrant dried apricots, dense almonds...

Jacob didn't hear Miriam approach until she was standing just inside the doorway, smiling at him. He could see her short plump figure, her greying hair escaping from her black scarf. Her fawn dress, with sparse thin orange stripes, contrasted with the dark tent walls. He quickly shut up and turned away.

'A chip off the old block! That's what yer is. Just like yer muvver, bless her! "Where are you, God?" Miriam laughed as she imitated Jacob's mother, Rebecca, with her high pitched voice. 'If I heard 'er say that once, I heard 'er say it hundred times! Like when she couldn't get pregnant. "Where are you God? How are we supposed to have many hoffspring if you make me barren?"'

Jacob let his sulky back give the message that he was too old, at fifteen, to be jollied along.

Miriam paused, and her tone was more conspiratorial, enticing. 'Yer know, I've wondered about that too. Why make 'em wait to 'ave the two of you? Maybe the One wanted 'em to have lots of pleasure in the trying, yer know?' Miriam chuckled and raised her eyebrows. 'Lots o kissin and cuddlin and the rest before the two of yer come with all yer arguments. Yer can have a lot o pleasure over twenty years!'

Jacob reddened. The servant was going too far, as usual. But she was more like an aunt in the family than a serving girl who could be rebuked and dismissed. Jacob put up with it.

'Now, there are people what think God was waitin fer Isaac to ask 'im proper for children.' Miriam continued her flow with no prompting. 'It's true 'e made a public thing o it. I can remember 'im at that sacrifice, standin over the smoke, telling The One that since 'e had given 'im a good wife, it were about time 'e give them children as well. 'E wasn't goin to use a maid to grow 'is seed. No way! If them others wanted that sort o strife, let them have it. No slave sons, thank you!

'Our Becs was touched, ohh, so touched. Tears in 'er eyes, poor thing. Havin 'im say she was a good wife, public, like that, when people naturally thought there was somethin wrong with 'er. Oooh, they was so close, yer Mum and Dad.' Miriam stood pensively for a moment. Jacob suspected that she was about to say 'Until you two came along…' but had thought better of it. Now his face was no longer burning, he turned to face the old family servant.

'Anyway. "Where are yer God?" are yer muvver's words.

It's good to 'ear you've picked that up from 'er! It weren't any different when she was pregnant. "Oh God," she groaned "where are you? They're tearing me apart them two inside! What's going on? How can I live if it's just going to be like this?' Miriam was enjoying her loud caricature of her mistress and friend. She sat down on a barley sack to the left of Jacob, who was now sitting upright on the hay.

'But with 'er, bless 'er,' Miriam continued more quietly, 'it's not just words. Some people shout and scream and make a fuss, vey say things about God but they don't mean 'em. They don't really wanna know where God is. Oh no! Far too scary, far too spooky. They wanna complain and look a little religious and make it all out to be 'is fault. They never actually wan' an answer. Your muvver did wan' an answer.' Jacob showed in his attentive face that he was enjoying story time. Miriam was not often one to recount a story, not one of the noted tale-tellers at feasts, so she enjoyed having an audience.

'She 'ad 'er own way o' asking God proper. Not when she was 'et up. Not at all. She kept the question and when things, you two mostly, had quieted down, she told me to say she was sleeping and not to be disturbed. She went and had a proper conversation. I don't know quite where she went. I think it changed. Sometimes she was gone longer than others. When she came back, she was more settled. She seemed to have got what she wan'ed, or needed. I didn't always know what it was. Except when it was about you two.'

'Anyways, the point of all this is, it's good to hear yer now saying "God, where are you?" Just take it serious. Treat it as a proper question, not just a rant.' Miriam smoothed her apron and looked around with her, 'Now what did I come in here for?' look.

Rather than be alone when Miriam found the next task, Jacob asked, 'Miriam, auntie, will you tell me again what Mum heard?'

'Well…' Miriam looked quizzically at Jacob, like the look she used to give him to see if he had washed properly. 'Yes,' she nodded to herself. 'I'm sure yer remember, don't yer...?'

Jacob shook his head trying to look ignorant.

'Let me see… What did she say? "Two nations is inside you, struggling; two peoples to come from you, rivals." Ye're important, Jake, ye're goin to be father of a nation! What's happenin or not happenin now don't matter. It'll happen. Sometimes it takes a long time, that's all. It seems to be 'is mysterious way!' Miriam looked up and smiled.

'Go on,' said Jacob. 'I'm sure Mum said there was more than that.' This was a little devious. He was giving the impression that his mother had told him more. Actually, he had heard it from Miriam without Miriam knowing. She had been telling off Esau for bullying his little brother and didn't know Jacob was listening. She had told Esau more of the prophecy. Now Jacob wanted her to tell him properly.

'Did she then? Well, she can tell yer 'erself if she wants.'

'Miriam,' Jacob coaxed, 'you know you've started, and you know what you say about that!' Miriam often said 'People who start and don't finish are worse than useless!'

Miriam frowned and looked around. Then she bent closer to Jacob. '"One'll be stronger than tother; the elder the younger serves."

'Are you sure that's what was said?' Jacob was puzzled.

'Why? O' course. The elder the younger serves. The elder becomes the servant o' the younger. Now you really do 'ave to wait for that one, little man! Just bide yer time and yer'll see.'

'That's what I thought it meant,' Jacob's face was still puzzled. 'But 'The elder the younger serves,' couldn't that mean the other way round? The younger serves the elder? That would be more normal.'

'Cheer up little man! Yer fink too much. The One knows what 'es about. You'll see. No good comes o' interfering in 'is ways.'

Miriam brushed her hands and lifted her head, eyes searching. Her mouth opened wide and her eyebrows raised as she reached out for the stock of spun thread. 'Now, there's just enough time for mendin yer dear muvver's pilla. It's no' a weapon you know!' Miriam frowned at Jacob and bustled out.

Jacob smiled to himself.

'Give me some.' Esau nodded at the stew Jacob was stirring. Jacob stared back at his brother's bent forehead, waiting for Esau to look at him.

Mostly Jacob was happier when Esau did not look at him. Esau's well-groomed black beard and hair surrounded a broad flat face with small, beady, eyes. These mean eyes looked down at Jacob; Esau a little over six foot, more than six inches taller than Jacob. Esau held himself upright with ease, his broad back, shoulders, chest, thick arms, all packed with muscle. Jacob only stood fully upright when he remembered to. His body hadn't swelled, not yet demanding new bigger clothes. His muscles kept themselves discreetly hidden. Most of the time, in the tents, swaggering felt out of place. Esau's hunting life was all about swagger, asserting power over the chosen victim from the start. In song, Esau was a stallion. Jacob saw him with the teeth and claws of a lion. And the speed. After being outrun by Esau twice, and bruised badly for his attempted escape, Jacob learned to avoid or demur to his twin. Now, at seventeen, Jacob's defiance was sullen and glowing and hidden.

'That red stuff.' Esau jerked his head towards the large pot.

'What?' asked Jacob gently, innocently.

'Red stuff!' Esau shouted. People could hear three tents away. The older children later started calling him 'Red Stuff.' It stuck.

'Red stuff!' Esau jabbed the air towards the pot. 'For me.' He glared at Jacob and jabbed both hands towards himself. 'To eat.' He chomped the air. 'I'm starving and you have red stuff. Hand it over.'

This was not the first time that Jacob felt Esau was talking to him as he would to his heel. Esau didn't really see the need to talk at all. His heel should know what he wanted and just do it. Like when he needed some warm water to wash his hands of the blood from his hunting kills. Jacob enjoyed being in the cooking tent, near his mother, and when he was young it didn't occur to him that he shouldn't do what the young women around him did so readily. When his brother first asked, politely, he had fetched the water. Later he could see Esau smirking and he realised that he was the only boy fetching washing water. It became a habit, which Esau insisted on. Recently, seventeen-year-old Esau had taken to just looking at Jacob, tilting his forehead back with a short sharp peremptory gestured order. Mostly Jacob complied. What else could he do? Then he took himself for short stompy walks, until his mother asked him what the matter was.

'Wait, Jakey. Don't be so impatient,' his mother would say. 'You're on the better path, can't you see? In the camp with the stores and the people and the trading. There's far more here in the end than out there with the animals and the bushes and the dust. Let Esau have his thrills, his kills, his man-slaps. He likes to be so big, such a man! What is he really learning about life, except go for it and kill it? You're heading for so much more than that, Jakey. Be patient. You have to wait for the seed to grow. Just let it happen even when you can't see anything. It'll grow. In God's time, it will, Trust me.'

Jacob's father was not interested. When Jacob stomped past him, he merely raised his thick eyebrows and sometimes even chuckled. Jacob then tried to shoot him with fierce eyes. Sometimes his father stopped chuckling, but he kept smiling. Jacob didn't like his father chuckling in derision. He heard the guffawing when Esau told his hunter's tales. He saw the beam on his father's face when he ate the venison. He longed for some scrap of this goodwill to fall over him. But he wasn't noticed and the longing in his eyes was brushed away with the command to 'Cheer up! The sky's not fallen yet.'

Jacob knew he couldn't complain to either parent about Esau treating him like a heel. But he couldn't just let Esau get away with it. This was extreme, even for Esau, on another level of nasty. Jacob didn't want his brother to think he could carry on at this level.

'OK, OK. You're hungry.' Jacob looked at Esau. 'How much?'

'As much as the greatest hunter needs! As much as these legs will take! Just one bowl to start with. And we'll take it from there.'

Jacob shook his head slightly and smiled warily. 'That's not what I meant. How much… will you give for your food?'

Esau looked blankly at him and then spoke emphasising each word, with pauses for extra emphasis. 'You… want me… to pay… for food…? Look Jakey, there are three carcases out there, big ones, enough to feed the whole camp for weeks. That's my contribution. Since when have you got on your high horse and decided that the whole way this family works is going to change? You do what you do with Mum and you keep me going so I can keep the family going. You… give me… the food!'

Jacob blinked and winced at Esau's tirade. He turned to the stew and stirred it. Was Esau going to grab a bowl and fill it? Jacob could see himself shouldered out of the way, helpless. Better to keep talking. 'It's just that it's not time yet. I'm sure everyone is looking forward to sitting down with you and eating with you. I don't think Mum would like you eating before everyone else.'

'Stop hiding behind Mum!' growled Esau. 'She won't know. I can eat now and eat with the others.'

'She was here just now,' said Jacob trying to keep calm. 'She knows exactly how full this is. She will see what you've taken out. She will know.'

'O for crying out loud! You and your stupid games!' Esau changed his voice to sound mocking, patronising. 'So little Jakey is playing at being salesman today. What a nice game! He has such a funny imagination. Oh Mr. Salesman, how much is that lovely. lovely, stew of yours?'

'It's... err... no ordinary stew, this one,' said Jacob nodding and trying to look shrewd. He needed time to work out how far he could go. 'See this colour? Have you ever seen a red so strong? This is no ordinary colour. This makes you ready for anything! Whoever eats this superlative red stew will have strength and wisdom for years to come.' Jacob smiled tentatively at Esau. 'Once you eat this red stew, your body will be so fit, you will live rediculously well for a hundred years!'

Esau glowered. 'Just tell me how much!'

Jacob looked his brother calmly in the eye. He wanted to send him away with nothing, so he asked for something Esau would never give him. 'You can have this now and pay later. Your rights as the first born. That's what it will cost you.' The first born was the acknowledged leader, decision maker. The first born received a double inheritance, twice as much as other sons.

'Look, I'll die if I don't eat now.' Esau opened his eyes wide and ogled the stew. 'What use are my rights as firstborn if I never live long enough?'

Jacob hid his surprise. 'That's the deal, then?'

Esau nodded in exasperation, gesturing for Jacob to hand over the stew.

29

'You swear?'

'I swear.'

'What do you swear?'

Esau snorted, returning to his patronising voice. 'For my little brother Jakey, I swear to give him my rights as firstborn, so that he will hand over this stew.' He glowered. 'Now!'

Jacob quietly handed over the lentil stew, with bread, and water. He refilled the bowl when Esau handed it to him. Esau wiped his lips with his hand, belched, stood up and swaggered out.

Chapter Two

Upheaval

(Genesis 26:1-6)

Jacob looked gloomily round the store tent. No heap of fragrant grass, no succulent dried fruits. A few old sacks of flour, dirty and leaking. Half a sack of beans. He knew there was far from enough for the months ahead. He knew how dry the land still was, even the valleys yellow brown rather than green, their streams a distant memory.

The older men argued about whether this was worse than the famine in grandfather Abraham's time. Jacob was slightly reassured that the family and entourage had come through something similar. But, in all his twenty-two years, he had never seen the land so empty, so aching. He wondered how and if they could come through.

Even Esau seemed defeated. At first, he had simply walked further, boasting, on his return with a gazelle carcase, of the huge hills he had conquered. Now he knew there was no point in exploring; he would run out of supplies, with nothing to forage. He did shoot the occasional pigeon which he ate by himself, sharing a leg, sometimes, with his father.

At first, too, Jacob had been pleased to see the stores come into their own. With the hunting so meagre, it was obvious why reserves were worth keeping. He even felt more important than his bigger brother. Now that the stores were depleted, Jacob was dejected. No-one could feel important against the relentless onslaught of dry dust.

Where was God? Why had The One withdrawn his blessing? This was the land that Grandfather Abraham had been led to by the One. Surely, he could provide for the family whom he had called now they were here? Had he turned his back on them? For what reason? Had his father done something to anger The One?

Jacob was proud that he had remained loyal to the family and their ways, despite some enticements from a couple of young women of neighbouring tribes. With Esau's birth-right, he was more attractive.

Later on red stew day Esau had complained loudly and bitterly about the trick Jacob had played on him and told their father over the meal that it was childish nonsense. Isaac hadn't laughed, for once, but had shaken his head seriously. 'You swore an oath, my son. Can you unsay those words?' Isaac had lifted his right index finger to emphasise the point. 'Words matter. The One is faithful; we have to be faithful. Say what you mean and mean what you say. Fulfil your oaths, however much it might cost you. Trust that The One will bring good from being faithful even in mistaken oaths, even in trickery.' Isaac had singled Jacob out with a silent stare of his large eyes, nodding his head slowly to say

'Yes, I mean trickery by you.' Jacob had known his father was not pleased with him, but that was the end of it. Part of Jacob was ashamed at his father's disapproval but part of him was proud at what he had achieved. Surely, if his father had deemed it that bad, he would have done more about it? Fathers are supposed to chastise their wayward sons and one hard stare hardly counted as chastisement.

Five years on, everyone knew Jacob had secured the birth-right and his conscience did not trouble him. What was it, then, that had made The One withdraw his blessing? Or was it just the family now going through what Grandfather Abraham had gone through, for some mysterious purpose?

Would they move? When and where? Jacob heard some of the advice his father was given. For almost a year there was general agreement that they needed to hold their ground, dry as it was. They knew they were in the land where The One wanted them to be. Jeshach, Isaac's portly chief steward, had been the first to broach the possibility of moving ('just a flying of a kite, sir, an exercise in considering all eventualities…) Amos, a wiry herdsman whose views Isaac valued, was adamant this was close to blasphemy ('woe, indeed, woe, to those whose loyalty to The One vanishes with the dew!')

Jeshach continued to highlight the economic plight of the family. They were buying more from Philistine traders, at higher prices. Reserves of silver and gold, as well as foodstuffs, were lower than for many years. He made no recommendation, only reported, repeatedly.

Jacob was aghast at the prices now being charged. 'We're slowly being sucked dry, killed off, Jeshach! And you tell them how grateful we are.'

Some Philistine traders had just left and Jacob was livid. 'You could have tried harder to bargain them down. Every bean counts for us now.'

Jeshach was sitting to Jacob's right, on a stone a little lower than Jacob's, his head only slightly higher than Jacob's. As they watched the traders leave from the rise to the west of their camp, Jeshach had sighed and suggested they take a few moments to sit together. He laid his elbow height staff, made from a single slim coppiced branch, with a bulbous top, on the ground beside him. He smoothed the folds of his dark blue robes over his calves.

Jacob looked back at the dun linen tents behind him, flapping lazily as the wind played with them. He wasn't keen to go back to the difficult daily decisions about how much of the stores could be eaten, to the looking in hungry, almost accusing, eyes. He sat down too. The circles of rough thorny branches, pens for the cattle, the sheep and goats, were to his right, downwind. They looked too large now for the thin animals the family had left. Jacob was hungry too, and angry.

'With respect, sir,' countered Jeshach smoothly, 'the prices on which we agreed, after appropriate negotiation, were only a little in excess of the prices of two months ago, despite the worsening climatic situation and the corresponding increasing demand from the residents of an increasing area.' Jeshach beamed as usual, ivory teeth framed by a closely trimmed light brown beard. The beard too was drier, less oiled, than before, and Jacob thought Jeshach's pronounced cheeks a little thinner. His continuing cultured cheeriness seemed out of place in the scorching struggle for survival.

'They want to see us gone. They're just extorting all they can before we have to leave.' Jacob glared in the direction of the departing traders. 'We need to put up more fight!'

'With continuing respect, sir, though I would agree that they are willing to benefit from our distressing current circumstances, as is normal in the ebb and flow of trade, they also have a settled awareness that they need our supplies as much as we need theirs. These hills are not to their liking, too isolated and arduous. But they much appreciate our meat, our fruits, our honey. They consider our beloved peaks and valleys a dangerous rabbit warren where they are quite happy for newcomers of all kinds to try to establish a home. If they can access the produce of the hills without the precipitous paths, they are content. And if they find a family whose measured produce is, shall we say, more consistent, they are willing, within the bounds of current market valuations, to encourage and support that family. Hence, you find that the increase we have suffered is markedly lower than that exacted on some of our more short-termist neighbours.'

'You mean that they charge us less because we swindle them less? You've just swallowed their empty flattery. Blood suckers!' Jacob spat out his words. 'I would almost be happy to see Esau hunt them down and take back their blood money.'

'I consider that you, sir, are a better man that that.

Intemperate violence always leads to pain and misery for the perpetrator.' Jeshach hectored. 'The severing of cordial relations for short term gain is always outweighed by the long term damage.' His loud words rang in the dry air.

Jeshach held up his hand to signal a brief silence. 'Our young master's perception is precise, though, on the most salient point,' he beamed and spoke with all his usual smoothness. 'We are paying out a considerable amount. How long can this continue?'

Three months later, after another failure of rain, Rebecca invited Jeshach and Amos to join her husband and sons for the last of their mint tea. The invitation was for early on a Monday morning, unusual for a social call. 'Tea to make you think, tea to help you talk,' Rebecca looked at them sharply. 'It's decision time, isn't it?' She bustled out back to her kitchen tent next door.

The men sat on low stools, set on a newly brushed old brown carpet with a few red and blue stripes. The tent walls were lighter, finer, than others in their camp. Bedding was rolled up at the bottom of the tent walls, some of it showing the red and green embroidery of the East, from where Grandfather Abraham had been called to travel.

The woman may have called the meeting but the participants were all men. Isaac, shorter than average, muscular, with large eyes and a confident, elegant, manner. Esau, tall, tanned and terrifically muscled, with wandering small eyes, restless, uncomfortable. Jacob, a similar height to his father, narrow-shouldered, thin, pale, with darting eyes, at times urgent and engaged, at others detached and distracted. Jeshach taller than average, slightly stout, with large, steady, eyes, upright, serious. Amos, the same height as Isaac, wiry, even more tanned than Esau, with piercing, small eyes in a sea of wrinkles and a determined, independent, even grim.

Jeshach set out the options. Amos was uncharacteristically quiet.

'I will try to be brief. This famine is being widely compared with the famine in the time of our much-missed pioneer and patriarch Abraham. Then he left the hills to which he had been led, conscious, in his own distinctive way, that this was the current, probably short term, will of The One. We could stay here and hope again for late rains soon. You will not be surprised that this is an option I do not recommend.'

Isaac nodded, downcast. Amos, remarkably, nodded too. 'I see them dried up valleys and I hear nothing. Nothing.'

'If I may continue,' rolled on Jeshach, 'I see good supplies among the Philistines. We have been paying a premium for delivery when animal fodder is more expensive that in the memory of most people. If we are to continue to subsist on Philistine produce, for whatever mysterious reason, we would lower our costs by moving, at least in that direction.' Jeshach paused for his words to sink in. 'Your father, sir, may have received similar advice, although I am well aware that his chief counsellor was far wiser, far longer-sighted, far more confident than any human.

'Most of the supplies in the hands of the Philistines

originate from Egypt, from the banks of the ever-flowing river. A viable alternative would be to make a longer journey to this well blessed origin. I have calculated that, if we were to depart within a week, we would be able to sustain the necessary lengthy journey and, thereafter, our prospects of earning a living through our labour would be substantial in an environment where our living costs would be considerably lower.

'Survival in order to return,' Jeshach nodded at Amos, 'is always our aim. A first sensible step, if I may suggest, would be to relocate temporarily to Gerar, where,' he turned towards Jacob, 'having cultivated good trading relationships, we are most likely to find a trustworthy welcome, or from where we could begin our trek to Egypt.' Jeshach sat back, his head erect, looking at the faces round him.

'Thank you Jeshach.' Isaac's voice was quiet, sombre. 'My father did indeed leave these hills of ours when necessary. Maybe it is time to follow his example. Sad.' He shook his head.

'There are other places, you know!' Esau's voice was angry, combative. 'We came from the East and now you want to take us further West. We'll be trapped, not able to come back, hemmed in by the sea. There are better lands where we came from, people more like us. Maybe a little longer journey, but then our options are more.'

'I know what you mean lad,' came Amos' slow serious voice. 'I just don't think we can make the Euphrates, not how we are, not without severe losses.'

'Most of us, the fittest, can make it at least to beyond

Damascus. Then we'll find enough to push through to Mum's family. Surely,' Esau looked round, 'it's better to get help from family, than from the Philistines!'

Jacob wondered if Esau had been talking to their mother. She had often spoken of how close she was with her brother, Laban, and what a good valley he lived in. Jacob wondered about agreeing with Esau, but he was too used to taking a different point of view from his brother. He kept quiet, as usual.

Jeshach looked encouragingly at Amos who turned to Esau. 'Three months ago, I would have gone with you. Not now.' He shook his head dismally. 'Too late.'

Jeshach cut in. 'The example of your esteemed father, sir,' a nod to Isaac, 'and the indubitable blessing which resulted from that temporary relocation, are stronger indications than relying on the resources of a homestead of limited means, even one presided over by kin. Part of the previous blessing was, may I remind you, that not one of us perished. The whole company was eventually able to return to our hills. Your plan, sir,' a half bow towards Esau, 'envisages, you say, a number of the "less fit" falling by the wayside? I submit that this is not an eventuality for which we should be preparing.' Esau glowered and kept quiet.

'Thank you, gentlemen, for your contributions.' Isaac seemed not have noticed Jacob's lack of contribution. 'We seem to have no workable alternative to Gerar for now. Knowing that I tread the same road as my father will be a comfort to me, and, I hope, to others. We will see what the One will do for us there!' Isaac's bright voice tried to inject some hope. 'We may also not be there for long. Whether we find a more permanent sanctuary in Egypt,' turning to Jeshach,' or with Laban,' turning to Esau, 'we shall see. We'll be nearer to the Way of the Sea, either South to the Nile or North and East to the family. Who knows how long we'll be in Gerar?'

Much dust flew up and around as the tents were untethered. A couple of servants were sent ahead with a few gift animals, seeking, preparing for, a welcome. No news would be good news. Only if the codes of hospitality were being set aside would the shocking message of refusal return.

Isaac's score of family, servants, families of servants, moved slowly, at the pace of the weakest. For half the journey a long straggle weaving down brown valleys. Harsh crow voices instead of the gentle chirrups of small birds. Then bunched together as they stepped out onto the edge of the coastal plain. Already here were strips of green where the last waters from their hills had been held in dark soil rather than being wastefully let go by rock.

The twin towers of the Great Gate of Gerar were first spotted from a little ridge four miles from the city. The walls stretched out from the Gate enclosing what looked like a great decapitated ant heap.

'It's huge,' exclaimed Jacob.

'Decidedly one of the largest cities in the region,' nodded Jeshach. 'One might fit 50 large vineyards within those walls, or 3000 of our livestock pens.' Jacob wondered if he was exaggerating for effect. He couldn't see the end of the city so maybe Jeshach's assessment was actually conservative.

The company stopped and caught up with each other, brushing off dust, sorting the animals into neater, separate, herds.

The towers on either side of the gates were indeed more massive than Jacob had ever seen. Most of the company stayed outside the walls while Isaac and his right-hand men ventured in. Jacob looked at the well-equipped soldier-guards and thought how impossible it would be to escape.

'Welcome, welcome indeed!' boomed a large man with a bronze chain hanging from his neck across his chest. 'To see the son of Abraham the blessed brings joy to our family and our city! Would that my father could have savoured this event.'

'Abimelech, the joy is ours, to be greeted so warmly,' replied Isaac. 'My father spoke in glowing terms of the hospitality and the help from your father. I see that you are a true son.'

'Come in, come in!' boomed the king's voice again. The surrounding soldiers were now more relaxed. 'We are simply friends catching up. Let's not talk now about who is helping who at this unusual time. Circumstances have drawn us together and we will enjoy the company!'

Water, bread and dried fruit were taken to the company huddled outside while Isaac and his party were ushered into the king's reception rooms for a meatier meal. To Jacob the welcome was extraordinary, too effusive, maybe not to be trusted.

'Why are you asking my advice?' cajoled Rebecca. 'Don't you have enough advisors? Aren't your man minds far-seeing enough?'

The family were in their main room in the sunny, hot, side of a small courtyard belonging to Phicol, one of Abimelech's generals. Up narrow crumbling steps from the opposite corner was a small old store room where the few sacks had been piled high to one side to make space for Rebecca to sleep. The main room was for the men and Rebecca seemed to enjoy her night-time, elevated, status. Now the bedding was rolled up by the wall and the family was sitting on the carpet, eating more bread and seeds with a few dried apricots.

'Rebecca, my lovely!' riposted Isaac. 'Do you really just want to do what you're told?' He laughed and their sons laughed along.

'Back to your brother, surely?' Esau's had stopped laughing before the others were ready.

Rebecca swayed her head in indecision, her eyes bright and her mouth closed.

'Do you think there will be better than Egypt?' Isaac's voice was strangely serious. 'Jeshach says Egypt is closer and more prosperous. He thinks we can learn some useful skills.'

'Oh yes indeed, esteemed, most exalted, sir.' Rebecca laughed along with her imitation of Jeshach. 'The most constant, most surging, most bounteous Nile provides a veritable cornucopia of prime produce to supply the needs of both the indigenous population and the surrounding peoples. Yet only a small fraction of that plentiful produce is able to be transported great distances, with the carriage costs making it produce of premium price. And the aforementioned indigenous population, with a laudable human aspiration to provide a more comfortable life for their offspring, are more than ready and able to engage other people to carry out the more basic tasks of a civilised life.' She drew breath, signalling the approaching climax of her peroration. 'So, sir, if I may draw some natural conclusions and suggest, merely suggest, some pointers. Our payments for provender, for simple sustenance, will be considerably curtailed once we have completed our journeying. We will have open-ended opportunities to offer our labour, at first as husbandmen and very soon as tradesmen and skilled servants. We may well become involved in the construction of permanent dwellings, maybe even have the satisfaction of contributing to immense, long-lasting, world-renowned construction projects. So much we can learn for the development of our own life!' Isaac began to applaud. Rebecca held out her hand to curb the premature enthusiasm. 'Your esteemed father sojourned among the Philistines and was able subsequently to resume his blessed residence on better foundations and better equipped and with better local relationships. How much more might our company benefit from a similar sojourn in an even more civilised environment? You may not be a Pharaoh, sir,' Rebecca bowed low with extravagant arm gestures, 'but I envisage you as the most sophisticated, the most experienced, the most wise leader in the whole of this world!'

The applause unleashed was loud and long. 'Mum, even Jeshach couldn't...' began Jacob also loudly.

'Shhh! Auntie!' Rebecca was urgent, almost cross. 'Remember who I am here!'

'You're a marvel!' called Isaac smiling broadly. 'Dear "sister". How much of Jeshach's real words did you hear, we wonder?' Rebecca pulled an aggrieved face. 'You can outtalk the talker! You can also outthink. So... do you think we'll return from Egypt better for the experience?'

'Or better from your home country?' Esau's eyes flashed as he made his view known again.

'Maybe it's Jeshach himself who would be the chief beneficiary of his civilised Egypt.' Rebecca's voice was more serious. 'Though I can't see him constructing anything other than longwinded advice. He'd look to fit in higher up the scale, among people more of his own kind.' Isaac nodded seriously too.

'So we head in the other direction!' Esau was sensing the wind blowing more at his back.

'It's a small, meagre, place for all of us,' said Rebecca sadly. 'And far.'

'So...?' Isaac puckered his face and lifted his hands with the urgency of a decision that had to be made.

'So why ask me? Do you think I can see into the future? For all I know it may be best to stay here. Why ask your sister, as though you don't have a wife?' Rebecca shot Isaac an annoyed glare. 'Don't you have another advisor?'

Isaac shook his head dismally.

'Another advisor with a much higher point of view, the one and only advisor in the end? Didn't your, sorry our,' Rebecca grinned, 'didn't our father say he should have listened more to God and less to his wife?'

Isaac looked down, put in his place. The boys were quiet.

Rebecca smiled. 'Yes, where is The One when you need Him? I'm sure you can find Him, or He can find you.'

Isaac nodded, uncertain. He shone a bright smile at Rebecca. 'Best of all women. And I thought I married you for your good looks!'

'Shh!!' said all three of the others at once.

A week later the inner council met again, in the hot room, this time with Jeshach and no Rebecca. They all wished they could just pull up a wall and let in a breeze. Esau fidgeted most.

'You know our sister Rebecca "suggested" in her unique way that I seek a higher authority?' Everyone smiled. 'Well. She also suggested I went up to her room one evening, on my own, away from it all. I wasn't sure what I was supposed to do there.

'She would have asked The One straight, so I thought I'd follow her example. "So!" I looked up, talking to the roof and beyond, I hoped. "Where do you want us for now? Egypt seems the best prospect."

'Nothing came. I knew she wouldn't be pleased if I came down in less than two hours. So, I thought I might as well relax and doze. No point in getting stressed.'

The others nodded their heads.

'It was pleasant up there, not too hot then, children's playing voices not too far away. I think I did drift off for a bit. Then one of the sacks seemed brighter. I rubbed my eyes and looked again. One standing sack was brighter and the one lying in front of it also bright. It was like a light was sitting there, leaning back. The air felt thicker, somehow, even more relaxing. The light had legs, feet and arms, hands. Not sure about a face. I looked and blinked and looked. Weird but good.

'Words came to mind. Like my words, but calmer, steadier, wiser. They seemed important enough to speak out. "Do not,' came first. I thought this would be "Do not fall asleep again!" I said it again "Do not … go down." I wasn't thinking of going downstairs. After a little pause the words came again, more now. "Do not go down to Egypt. Settle in the land which I will tell you."

'Was I advising myself? It felt like the light-person was advising me and using my voice. Talking about it now, the strangest thing was that it didn't seem strange. I was relieved to have one option removed.

'"Stay a while in this land and I will be with you and will bless you." That seemed to remove the family option too. Stay put, blessing will come here. There was more.

'"This land, all these lands, I will give to you and your descendants." I was still speaking out words that came, not quite realising what I was saying. 'And I will fulfil the promise I made to your father Abraham. I will make your family a large family, with many descendants, as many as there are stars in the sky. And I will give your descendants all these lands. And all the nations of the world shall find blessing through your descendants. Because Abraham did what I told him, obeying my voice as obeying an instruction, a command, a law.' A lot of "ands." The main thing is that we're staying here for now. We've been told.' Isaac seemed relieved.

'That's him, that is,' said Amos. 'He can be direct, to the point, and he also likes to talk about the big picture. Plenty of hope there, that's his way.' Amos still sounded dismal. 'Ah but you have to do what he says, like old Abe. Even if it feels like killing your family!'

'For now, it's more what we don't do.' Isaac tried to lighten the mood. 'Don't go to Egypt! Just don't go there! We don't have to do anything, just

don't leave, for now.'

'The voice does indeed sound like the voice which guided your great father,' said Jeshach, ruminating out loud. 'The same promise, the very same! There is blessing here, somewhere.' He looked around. 'Our challenge is to trust that this comparatively poor environment can sustain all of us. But I think I detected a future importance in us making this our home for now, in the repeated promise that all these lands will be those of your descendants, sir. The impression I have, which may be a distorted impression, and needs to be assessed by closer, calmer, examination of your words, sir, is that our staying here is a means of enlarging the territory of your descendants from the bounds originally assigned to your father. Remarkable!'

The others seemed at a loss for words.

'Let's pass on the good news,' cheered Isaac. 'The One says our blessing is here, so we're staying!'

CHAPTER THREE

A Blessed Life

(Genesis 26:1-15)

Gerar was an outpost of Philistine territory, a walled town on the Eastern side of the coastal plain away from the main Philistine trading ports. Gerar meant 'Town of Jars', a good depot for produce drawn in from further inland and for goods sold in exchange.

News of the extreme drought had arrived in the town early. A small consortium of merchants had swiftly chartered a ship from their partners on the coast to carry out as many jars, bowls, knives, combs, necklaces, belts, as possible, and to return with as much wheat, barley, wine, pulses, nuts and dried fruit as possible. The town was well able to help outsiders, at a price.

Buying and selling, as well as simple food processing, with a little manufacturing, were the strengths of the Philistines. They lived by accommodating to the needs of the river of travellers who passed along their 'Way of the Sea' highway connecting the great Empires birthed by the

Nile and the Euphrates, as well as to the needs of the other trading ports in the Eastern Mediterranean. Anything, everything, could be bought and sold. Wine, beer and olive oil were plentiful. The gods and feast days and fertility rites of all their trading partners were honoured. All the physical needs of men away from home comforts were humoured and exploited.

Jacob was not alone in being suspicious, at least, of the Philistines, their many gods and movable morals. Isaac was afraid that the striking Rebecca, hips swaying under dark waving hair as she walked to market, would be a target for a local big man, for his pleasure or trade. As her husband, he too considered himself a target. Knowing that her family were far away, a ruthless Philistine could dispatch him, secure her, and count on few reprisals. Better, he decided quickly on the day they arrived, that, for the Philistines, Rebecca was his sister, with an extended family close by to deter poaching. Isaac had not thought this through, nor discussed it. He had known that his father had followed the same stratagem in the same circumstances in Egypt, and in Gerar, years before and he copied his father automatically.

'I'll take on anyone who tries!' challenged Esau, aggrieved. 'Let them know she has a son to stand up for her. There'll be no nonsense!' Esau did not push hard. He did not want his father to dwell on him being far more physically able to protect his mother than his father could protect his mother, years before. Jacob again felt overlooked. Didn't she, they, have two sons?

'Mum,' Jacob called quietly when she was cooking one day, 'It doesn't seem fair or right. Dad talks about always telling the truth and then makes us lie every day! Does it really help you, or anyone?'

'Sisters have brothers. Sisters can call for help. Sisters need to be paid for. But widows? Who cares for the widows?' Rebecca shook her head in sorrow. 'Besides, he's only copying his father.'

'But didn't Grandad Abraham rent Grandma out to Pharaoh?' Jacob sounded aghast.

'How did you know that?' shot back Rebecca.

'Dad laughed about it once, ages ago.' Jacob frowned. 'Laughing about how the blessing from The One keeps coming despite dodgy decisions. Even though Grandad sold his wife for Pharaoh's pleasure, she came back to him before long with a huge 'dowry' from the big man. Set him up for life. Ha… ha…' Jacob was not laughing.

'Not the best time in Grandma's life.' Rebecca paused, shaking her head. 'I think these people are more respectful. And I'm making it known that my nephews will fight for me.'

'Did Grandad do the same here too? I heard something about that as we approached this place.' Jacob frowned. 'I can't believe he would have done it again?'

Rebecca's sigh was long and deep. She nodded. 'Grandma was also a 'guest' of the last Abimelech, father of this one.'

'Good grief!' Jacob shook his head. 'How did she escape?'

'The One had to step in, bless him.' Rebecca looked up.

'He made Grandad change his mind?' hoped Jacob

Rebecca shook her head. 'He seemed to think it easier to lean on the Philistine king.'

Jacob was puzzled at The One being more able to speak to a Philistine. 'How did He make that pagan change his mind?'

'You know they are happy with many children from many women. He stopped that.' Rebecca raised her eyebrows.

'He stopped them sleeping together?' Jacob was incredulous.

'Well, He somehow kept the king away from Grandma,' smiled Rebecca. 'And for a few months no-one became pregnant. I expect they kept trying…' Rebecca winked.

'Really?' Jacob tilted his head, puzzled. 'If the other women weren't producing, wouldn't the king have wanted more to try a new one?'

'Who knows His ways?' The upward look again. 'How else to grab the man's attention? How else alert him that something's very wrong?'

Jacob still did not understand. 'How could he have known what the something was?'

'Aah! A dream!' Rebecca became the story-teller, arms waving, head tossing. 'Doom, death, disaster! That woman, the gorgeous new one. She is married! And you will die…'

'Was it his fault?' Jacob was beginning to feel sympathy for this Philistine. 'Hadn't he been misled?'

'That's what he thought. Protested his innocence.' Rebecca nodded, agreeing. 'But he had to let her go. And he had to ask Grandad to pray for him.'

'So he just released her quietly?' Jacob thought that was the end of it.

'Oh no,' Rebecca shook her head. 'The king called in Grandad in front of all his advisers. "What have you done? Why try to trap us into committing a sin? You have done what should not have been done!" '

'Good questions!' Jacob sounded brighter. 'Doesn't Dad need to hear this?'

'He knows, he knows…' Rebecca was despondent. 'He just thinks the One sorted it out. Whether it was right or wrong for Grandad to give up his wife, the One made it all come good, very good. A bit like Grandad giving up his son…'

Another question came quickly from Jacob. 'What good can come out of you being put at risk?'

'Oh, the usual. Sheep, cattle, men slaves, women slaves, and silver!' Rebecca sighed. 'Grandad benefitted in the end, though he would say all the family benefitted.'

Jacob's mind was finding all this hard to take. 'You don't think Dad is hoping for more of that?'

'Who knows what he sees ahead?' Rebeca shrugged. 'Does anything stop him laughing? But is it right to expect the One to step in every time?'

'Grandad doesn't seem as worthy of respect as we've been told,' challenged Jacob.

'Is anyone perfect?' Rebecca lifted her palms in front of her. Aren't we all a mixture? As long as we keep learning, including from our mistakes.'

'Dad seems to have learnt the wrong lesson!' Jacob emphasised. 'He can't repeat the same mistake trusting The One to just sort it out again.'

'Can't he?' Rebecca seemed calm. 'Who knows how

many times The One is prepared to cover our mistakes? I think it does help, though, for us to recognise the mistakes as mistakes.'

'Isn't it better for someone to step in? Let Abimelech know the truth.' Jacob felt ready for a fight.

'And how are you going to do that?' Rebecca's eyes narrowed. 'Do you think he'll believe you, rather than your father? And do you want to bring shame and division into the family?'

'We can't just do nothing!' Jacob clenched his teeth.

'Do you think you can tell your father off?' Rebecca suggested with a sigh. 'Might he listen to you? Is he open to what you have to say?'

'You know how little time Dad has for me,' Jacob's voice was gloomy. He paused. 'We'll just have to make sure you're safe.'

'Thanks.' Rebecca smiled. 'I know I can reply on my 'nephews.''

Jacob nodded. 'If only we could trust their morals more.'

'Their morals?' Rebecca challenged. 'Who says they don't behave better than us? They never so much as move a finger towards my bottom. Dad's saying to them "You can have her if you really want, just don't kill me for her" and they're behaving like gentlemen, really! I don't know where you get the idea that they can't control themselves.'

'Have you seen their sex obsessed idols and what they get up to in front of them?'

'You just keep your head high, your clothes sensible, your eyes meeting theirs. Do you think they have the guts

to take on a woman who'll talk them to death?' Rebecca
smiled proudly.

While the close family members lodged in the town where
King Abimelech could engage with them and keep an eye
on them, the rest of the company, with the animals which
remained, camped five hundred yards to the East. Living
in the direction from which they had come gave them the
sense that they could leave for home easily. They accepted
necessary supplies and kept their distance.

As expected, Isaac's company helped out willingly
and earnt their keep. Jacob worked in the store room and
counting house of an up-and-coming merchant. Esau
helped guard goods on the short journey to and from
Gaza on the coast and, sometimes, as far as the great port
of Ashkelon. Isaac's people drew water, washed clothes,
chopped wood, cleaned floors, made themselves useful.

Two years passed. A couple of children were born to
servants. But not enough rain fell to return to 'our hills.'
Jacob was often in the camp, either on business or visiting
Miriam. Nights spent in a tent, closer to his kindly 'auntie,'
with fewer voices arguing or singing or yelping nearby were
refreshing. They gave him hope of a soon return to clearer,
hilly, air.

One day, returning to town, on the alley leading to their
lodgings, he heard his father's laugh, louder than for a good
while. 'Wife! It's so good to get my hands on you!'

Isaac did indeed have his arms round Rebecca, though
still well above her bottom. 'The truth is out?' quizzed

Jacob. 'How did that happen?'

'Abimelech saw us this morning.' Isaac was smiling broadly. 'We just happened to be in his view when I let my hands say what my lips couldn't.'

'I hadn't felt so unsisterly in a long time!' chimed Rebecca. 'But did it just happen?'

'And it's all OK?' Jacob was worried. 'He took it OK that you'd been having him on?'

'I was summoned. A two-guard escort.' Isaac tried to sound serious despite his smile. He lifted his finger echoing the admonition of the king. '"She's your wife! I've just seen you. It's obvious." He wasn't pleased, but more aggrieved than angry. "And why did you tell us she's your sister?" '

'I had to tell him I thought I would die over her.' Isaac shook his hands in front of his chest, conveying the king's annoyance. "What is this you have done to us! It would have been so easy for someone to sleep with your wife! You would have brought guilt on us."

'Am I so easy then?' flared Rebecca.

'Abimelech has issued a decree. Anyone who touches me or my wife,' Isaac paused briefly, 'will face certain death. It's all worked out well!'

'With a bit of help,' Rebecca stage-whispered to Jacob. 'Did it just happen?' she repeated.

'Well, did it?' asked Jacob.

'Do you think it was just coincidence that this was in full view of the king's dressing room, shortly before his main morning audience?'

Jacob opened his eyes wide. 'So… you… got Dad to embrace you there?'

'You men!' laughed Rebecca. 'You think everything, or nothing, is your doing. Men don't even see how they can be led.' Rebecca lowered her voice again. 'If your wife, God bless her, ever tells you that her period is very heavy and going on a long time so that you miss the touch of her desperately, don't always believe her!' Rebecca laughed merrily.

'However it happened,' Isaac sounded chastened. 'it's all worked out well, thanks to The One.'

'And do you now think he can work things out without us having to tell lies?' stabbed Rebecca.

'Sorry,' Isaac raised his eyebrows and pulled a face like a child apologising while making light of his so-called misdemeanour.

'Yes! You are important to the plans of The One,' lectured Rebecca, 'but that doesn't mean that anyone who's not your son is dispensable.'

'Sorry.' Isaac's sorrow now sounded genuine.

The next day Jacob hurried back to the camp to tell Miriam and others the good, relieving, news.

'Oh my days! She's a one!' The pride was obvious in Miriam's voice. 'She took 'er time, but she knew when to make 'er move. Clever, clever, girl.' Miriam smiled as she shook her head.

'It does seem to mean that we're even more settled here, though,' said Jacob with some gloom.

'It's just not 'ome, is it?' Miriam mirrored Jacob's gloom. 'I pray and pray for rain, and it don't come. Not enough, anyways.'

'Keep it up, Auntie M! Where would we be without your prayers? You'll see it before too long.'

'Well, I don't see rain, but I do see somethin.' Miriam gave Jacob a gentle stare.

'Ah!' Jacob held her eyes with interest. 'And you see...?'

'Not rain but grain. Falling from the heavens like snow, it is. And not there,' Miriam looked up in the direction of their hills, 'here.' Miriam pulled in her chin with annoyance.

'Well, thanks to our hosts, we are OK with grain. Though they do make us work, and pay plenty, for it.'

'It's not on them, i's on us! I's only on our camp, and sort o thicker in that bumpy land other side from the town.' Jacob knew the place, lined with odd little ridges. 'Snake Trap' some of the locals called it. Early in the morning, mist collected between the ridges. No-one would walk there for fear of hidden snakes or spirits.

'That's a waste of a place!' Jacob was annoyed and urgent. 'Grain feeding the spirits, making them stronger, trapping us here! Keep praying M. Break the power of whatever is keeping us here.'

Miriam's grain picture stayed with Jacob as he returned home. Over dinner his Mum asked him, as she always did, how her old friend was, so Jacob told them glumly what she had seen.

'Grain from the heavens? You think that's bad? Why bad?' asked Rebecca.

'It's a haunt of spirits and snakes! It's going to them.' Jacob's annoyance conveyed how stupid he found the question.

Esau half nodded 'Avoid it. They'll trip you up.'

'We've started believing everything they say?' Rebecca gave a little, derisive, toss of her head in the general direction of the town. 'Was there anything bad coming out of that land? Don't you think the One would have shown her if it was a warning?'

Isaac coughed gently. 'You said she saw grain on our camp too? That doesn't sound so bad.'

Jacob kept a sullen silence. 'Carry on,' urged Rebecca to Isaac. 'What's that half smile about? You're not going to keep it to yourself, are you?'

Isaac smiled, relaxed, at his wife. 'I don't know how you know these things! I thought I was being serious.'

Rebecca raised her eyebrows at her husband and smiled back. 'Carry on!' she urged more.

'Sorry, Jakey, but it does make me smile. I've got a happy tickle inside. What if it is The One raining grain on us? He will provide!' Isaac was now chuckling again. 'I want to go and look at that land.'

'Go with him, Jakey, Esau,' said Rebecca gently.

A couple of days later. Isaac and Jacob were at Snake Trap. Esau had said he would come with them, but, apparently, an urgent opportunity couldn't be turned down. Something about Esau's licking of his lips made Jacob think there was a local woman involved.

'Come on!' urged Isaac to the hesitant, stationary, Jacob. 'The One made this land too, you know!' He walked along one little trough, then turned right and hopped from ridge to ridge. A few were regular, almost straight. Most petered out or joined other ridges. To Jacob it looked like someone had taken out their anger by messing up the earth's surface.

Isaac held out his arms and whirled round. He looked up to the heavens and shouted. 'Really?' Jacob was embarrassed and glad no-one was looking. 'Come on!' shouted Isaac again. Reluctantly, Jacob joined him on a ridge in the middle of Snake Trap.

'Do you have dreams?' Isaac looked at Jacob with a smile. 'Last night I saw two ships moving up and down here. I was on one and you were on the other – with quite a few of our other men.'

'Ships?' Jacob frowned.

'What brings us the grain?' countered Isaac. 'Something moving through the ground?'

'If it's ships, who says it's for us? We're not about to leave the land behind! They do ships, not us.' Jacob was cross and felt that he was fighting a losing battle.

'Anyone can do ships, they just have to learn,' replied Isaac patiently. 'But the ships mean something else that moves through the ground, which we don't do at the moment either?' Isaac waited for Jacob to answer.

Jacob shrugged and kept quiet.

'Ploughs!'

'You're not going to start growing grain? Here of all places?' Jacob tried to sound incredulous. 'Don't you want to be back on our hills?'

'I'm certainly thinking of it. The idea could be from him.' Isaac looked up and then looked at Jacob, questioning silently. 'These Snake Trap channels are just that. You can feel the ground is softer, wetter. And these ridges stop the whole place going boggy. I know nothing about ploughing and sowing. But, from the way our neighbours talk about it when I've been to their house for a meal, it was new to their grandfathers too, and now they do very nicely when the rain comes.'

Jacob shook his head silently.

'We'll see what your mother says.' Isaac strode back in her direction.

Rebecca didn't say much. 'Why not? What do you have to lose except a little time and effort? Haven't you decided already?'

Jeshach said little, for him. 'The prospect of producing our own provisions is pleasant indeed. Perhaps risky, perhaps making us a butt of unwelcome jokes, but no more than that. A development which a wise leader considers worth an attempt.' He too seemed to think that Isaac had decided already.

Amos too was, for him, notably positive. 'The One has all the land in his hands. I can see sweat; I can see waiting. I can't see disaster.'

The Philistines were more than happy to train Isaac and his men. Isaac's well-known friendship with Abimelech and the decree that he should not be harmed, meant that his subjects wanted to show their loyalty by being helpful. None of them went as far as stepping into Snake Trap, and a couple declined to let their oxen go there. But an army officer said his oxen were strong enough to cope with anything, and they could use his plough too. Isaac did wonder, out loud to the family, if Abimelech had had a word behind the scenes.

The training was over in a few days. Men used to controlling donkeys soon picked up the slower, heavier, hand needed with oxen. The Philistines talked a lot about the wrist action for broadcasting seed, the right angle, from the right height, with the right speed to penetrate the soil. But different people had different techniques, so Isaac and his men copied a little and thought they would just make it up as they walked along. Isaac had saved up enough money to buy a couple of sacks of seed. There was a general collection to buy two more sacks, which the locals said was too much for that odd piece of land.

Then they waited. Jacob had assumed they would start straight away when the lessons were fresh, but Isaac smiled and said 'No need to rush.' At the end of the second rest day after the training Isaac announced he and his little team were going to plough the next day. For the superstitious locals the moon was too clear. They thought a heavenly covering was needed.

Jacob was surprised to see a gaggle of Philistine boys running behind them as they drove the oxen to Snake Trap. Somehow the news was out and the tykes didn't want to miss seeing the hillbillies yelping and scarpering when their feet were gouged by the hidden, venomous, guardians of that land.

Isaac ploughed the first furrow, right in the middle of Snake Trap, along the bottom of a long trough. The small slopes helped keep the furrow straight. As he turned the ox round, he beamed at his handiwork. He then pulled the ox hard to left and ploughed up one side of the low trough. The ox kept trying to go back off the slope but Isaac kept yanking it back. This furrow weaved back and forth. In places the bottom of the trough was very well broken up. Isaac stopped for a quick drink, and headed back up the opposite side. This time his right arm had to work hard. At the end he turned round, wiped his forehead and beckoned for someone else to make the next furrow. Jacob thought he was looking at him, and he hesitated, still not quite convinced this was worth all the effort. Amos' young son, Caleb, ran forward and took control of the ox.

Isaac then walked back, ahead of Caleb and the ox in the next trough, back to where the little group was watching silently. He shouldered the seed basket and set off along his furrow. 'In you go! Get in there!' he shouted as he flung. He stopped and looked round a couple of times, beaming like a boy who has just learnt to spin a top.

Isaac didn't want to tire out the borrowed animal, so they stopped well before the sun was low. The local lads had long gone home disappointed, no drama in watching ploughing.

The job was done in a couple more days. Four days later, the next rest day, a cool breeze suddenly blew in the morning and by midday it was raining, on Isaac's seed. 'Beginner's luck!' Abimelech called it.

The rain wasn't enough properly to soak the ground. Some locals went out ploughing anyway, trying to catch the moisture, complaining that the top layer was slippery while the underneath was rock hard. Others waited for signs of more, prolonged, rain. They waited in vain. Only a few light showers came, spread over three weeks. Very little could germinate in this disappointing wet season. Isaac was glad the locals still didn't go near Snake Trap, as they would be jealous of the strong green shoots all along his natural troughs.

The second rains were similar, only tickling the tops of the half-grown Philistine barley, while landing more on Isaac's bigger leaves. No-one was surprised when, near the time for harvest, the sky was again cloudless. The Philistine scythes had soon cut their meagre crop before it withered completely. Isaac then had no trouble borrowing scythes and a couple of the more adventurous Philistines came along for on-the-job tutoring.

The Philistines stopped still in front of the thick undulating expanse of barley. They stared; mouths open. They looked at Isaac and his men with the unspoken question 'How on earth?'

Along the bottoms of the maze of troughs the grain had grown tall, with each head bending with the weight of seed. Even on the tops of the ridges, slightly less thickly, barley stood tall proudly presenting fully formed heads. As the breeze played, the barley rippled, the ridges so much like crests of waves that Jacob could imagine ships ploughing through.

Scythes proved not so effortless. The ridges hindered the usual swinging motion. The thick and close-packed stalks resisted the blades. One of the Philistines went back to Gerar to fetch more scythes and a sharpening stone. Isaac's people then swung at his harvest with joyful gusto. The amateur sowing had been so successful, that no-one was worried about amateur harvesting. The barley took 5 days to cut fully into very uneven sheaves. All enjoyed a satisfied rest day.

The sky stayed blue for the drying, winnowing,

threshing. The chaff blew away easily in the gentle breeze, seemingly glad to be released from the heavy kernels. The Philistines said they had never heard such thudding of weighty barley. Isaac had sown three and a half sacks of seed. He filled three hundred and sixty sacks, about a quarter of the available empty sacks in the whole town.

Every family had a couple of sacks for their own use. They also stored as many sacks as they could. Isaac's upstairs room was full to the ceiling. Jacob's employer stored the remainder. Jacob was happy now to be again store-keeper of their own produce.

'Beginner's luck' kept returning, as King Abimelech said often. His well-known good humour about Isaac's growing prosperity, and frequent invitations for Isaac to eat at the King's Table, stalled local jealousy.

Snake Trap proved again and again to be remarkably fertile land. Isaac again and again made inspired choices about what and when to plant. After the second very full harvest, Isaac looked out for other, unused, unwanted, land. More and more of Isaac's family company left or cut short their work for the locals. They tended pockets of land, small and large, some now sown with wheat, some with beans. They shepherded the sheep and goats, with a few cattle, brought with the bounteous barley bonus.

If the Philistines thought that Isaac was increasing his risk with his diversification, and would live to regret it, they were proved wrong, again and again. Barley, wheat, beans, sheep, goats and cattle all grew strong. Some Philistines kept a close eye on what Isaac was planting and copied. Their harvests were as ample as Isaac's.

After another two years of very full harvests, Isaac looked further 'afield' for suitable land. Esau continued to disdain the ripping open of earth that was meant for animals, and hunters, to roam. He could not see why anyone would want to tie themselves to one small square of earth when The One had given such expanses to explore. But he did mention a few places not too far away, including a couple near old wells dug by Grandad Abraham in his early wandering days. The wells had been filled in by the Philistines but were made usable with some hard work.

Isaac now rented his own house in Gerar. The company all had new or renewed tents. They walked tall in the market and bought from the quality stalls. Jacob was counted as one of the leading merchants. He employed a couple of the Philistine men alongside whom he had previously worked. He was invited to Merchants' Dinners. He was asked to invest in a couple of maritime ventures but this was a step too far for him, and for his father.

Now 28 years old, Jacob was thinking seriously about his future. Philistine friends asked if he would ever be allowed to settle down. The issue was not permission but place. Good though life was, Jacob still dreamed of a life in their hills, breathing fresher air, away from the confused and confusing voices of international trade, money and pleasure. He could not imagine settling anywhere else.

'You don't seem as keen as you were to go home?' Jacob eventually challenged his father one evening as they ate together.

Isaac looked up, frowning a little with surprise at the harsh tone.

Rebecca cut in 'Oh Jakey, what makes you say such things? Don't you see that all we buy is movable? Don't you hear the longing in your father's voice?'

Isaac nodded, smiling at his wife's apt words.

'But what are you waiting for?' Jacob pleaded. 'We have plenty, we can go home tomorrow!'

'He has a point,' conceded Esau. 'We'll turn to pillars of mud if we stay much longer.'

'Now here's a challenge!' smiled Isaac. 'The two of you on the same side, against me!'

Isaac paused and looked at his sons. They tried to avoid looking at each other.

'So?' attacked Esau.

'You haven't answered me, Dad,' pleaded Jacob.

'How do I know when to return?' Isaac chuckled. 'You know sometimes I think I'm becoming more like your mother, answering with a question.'

Rebecca shot her husband a warning look.

'You want to know the answer?' Isaac gathered breath to gather emphasis. 'The blessing! That's the most important thing in life.'

Esau rolled his eyes.

'Why would we move anywhere, when the blessing is with us here?' explained Rebecca. 'Why be impatient for what The One has promised us? What's wrong with enjoying the blessing here, now, and moving when the blessing fades?'

'The One is with me here,' confided Isaac, earnestly.

'You can't see him, you can only see the blessing, the harvests. But the blessing is what happens when he's around. Here and there, I sort of see him. Sometimes it's more of a feeling. He always seems relaxed, like he's staying for a while. He thinks he has everything under control.' Isaac shook his head and beamed again. 'Relax Jake, Esau, it'll all be fine.'

Both young men kept quiet, unsmiling.

'We'll have you eating Philistine salt fish before we leave!' joked Rebecca.

Esau huffed. Jacob called out 'Mum! Not that!' Isaac laughed 'Please, love, spare us!'

CHAPTER FOUR

Moving On

(Genesis 26:16-23)

The stores were spared attack by mould, rats, and thieves. Prices were good, especially at the times Isaac said to sell. More hands were needed and only Philistine hands were available. Locals looked after Isaac's animals; locals now drew water and made firewood and washed clothes for Isaac's people. Isaac was already one of the wealthy of Gerar. The sixth harvest was looking set to be at least as good as the previous five.

A leading member of a ship consortium came to dinner to cement a deal for part of Isaac's forthcoming harvest to be exported to Cyprus. Delshia and his assistants came in their third best robes, a sign that he saw Isaac as a friend as much as a formal supplier.

'People look at you with wonder!' Delshia stirred a generous dollop of honey into his mint tea after the food had been cleared.

'We look at ourselves with wonder,' mused Isaac with a smile.

'It's good that you want to share the blessing around. Everyone respects the support you give to widows, especially the sailor widows.' Delshia was looking more serious now. 'You can hardly be accused of only helping your own!' Even the adventurer Esau had stayed away from ever boarding a boat. The sea churned with too much chaos for any of Isaac's people to even go near. Partly because of this, they sympathised with those bereaved by the sea.

'Go on...' encouraged Isaac, inviting the real point of this preamble.

'It's just that not everyone rejoices at the good fortune of others. People can look at you and your great company and feel resentful. You and I know that your wealth has not been gained at the expense of anyone else.'

'Except that prices have been lowered by us flooding the market?' cut in Jacob.

Delshia laughed politely. 'The market is much wider than Gerar. Prices are set more by what happens in Egypt than by any local producer. As I was saying, not everyone understands how wealth grows through hard work and good fortune. Some think a rich man must have made other people poor. And, unfortunately, there are always some poor people.'

'And the poor who have been helped by outsiders can be embarrassed, at least?' ventured Isaac.

'And the locals can feel under more pressure to help their own poor,' sympathised Delshia.

Isaac shook his head. 'Envy is a terrible thing. So what do we do?'

'We can't change human nature,' challenged Jacob.

'Can't attack us. Not against their own king!' shot in Esau.

Esau pointedly turned to Delshia. 'Your advice is...?'

'My advice is to seek the King's advice.' Delshia was even more serious. 'An audience with Abimelech will not be difficult to obtain.'

When the trader and his assistants had left Isaac looked uncharacteristically sombre. 'So I have been summoned!'

Isaac and Jeshach were kept waiting. They could hear laughing in the King's Reception Room; the conversation topics were hardly pressing matters of State. No one offered them a drink. Finally, they were ushered in, trying not to look too disgruntled or afraid.

'Isaac, the blessed!' greeted Abimelech. He beamed at first but, after the greeting kiss, his face was solemn.' You are a big man now, far bigger than when you came to shelter under our wings. I swear your expert Advisor is twice the size of the man with loose grey robes who had trekked for hungry days to reach our open arms.'

Isaac nodded to Jeshach to reply. 'It is a wonder to us how all have prospered since your most gracious and generous welcome. We rejoice indeed at the new fields your people are cultivating with such skill and healthy reward, at the increased ship-loads with which you are able to provide for the peoples of many distant lands, at the proliferation of jars now fulfilling the promise of the name of Gerar, at the new wing to your esteemed palace which has, we hear, increased your esteem in the eyes of our neighbouring towns. It is indeed a joy to us to see the blessing come to you and your people. These years, ushered in by your open-hearted and public welcome, have been years of growth,' Jeshach, smiling, patted his ample belly, 'growth for all of us.' He ended flinging his arms wide open.

Abimelech nodded to his Advisor. 'Our wise and noble King Abimelech thanks you for your appreciation of the welcome he has extended to you, purely out of his generous nature. There has indeed been a change over the years since you arrived, a family battered by drought, carrying pitifully few belongings on your bony backs. We see that you are now no longer a family but a people. We see that you no longer own little, but enjoy great possessions. We see that you no longer need the gracious covering of our fathering King and his people, but you are strong enough to make your own way in the world.'

'Isaac,' added Abimelech with sincere open face. 'It's simple. You have outgrown your temporary place here. You're bigger than we are! Move away. You have grown with us, now grow away from us.'

'And you have grown...' began Jeshach before Isaac put a restraining hand on his shoulder. 'No point,' Isaac whispered.

'Yes, Abimelech,' rang out the friendly voice of Isaac. 'You want us gone, so we go!' He pulled Jeshach's arm. They turned and left without customary farewells.

'Why aren't you pleased?' Rebecca challenged Jacob. 'You were the one eager to move away from these corrupt people!'

'They're just kicking us out!' Jacob hit back. 'No thanks for virtually doubling their land under the plough. No thanks for showing them the benefits of a reputation for honest treading. No thanks for the blessing on them. Just "Get out, you strange wealth-suckers!" If that's how they see us, we'll show them. We can walk away with our sacks full of what they owe us.'

'We'll walk away with what is rightfully ours and not one bean more!' snapped Rebecca. 'Are we to become thieves now? Are we not in a better position than when we came? Are we to fleece them as though The One can't provide for us?'

'It's not right.' Jacob fought on. 'A parting of the ways negotiated with honour and mutual respect is one thing. An expulsion which makes everyone think we're undesirable is another. Who will welcome us, who won't pick on us, knowing how the Philistines have kicked us out? They'll just enjoy giving us more kicks.'

'Calm down,' pleaded Rebecca. 'We don't look like a bunch of vagabonds, not any longer. We're an impressive company. We can pay our way handsomely. Why shouldn't people respect what they can see with their own eyes?'

'And are you going to fight off the raiders with your own hands?' Jacob was a little calmer, but more pointed. 'Who will protect us from the likes of the Ishmaelites with their swords? Rich pickings, that's what we'll become.'

'Are we alone? Didn't we stay here because The One

told us to? I remember that not everyone was happy with that decision.' Rebecca's words hit their target. She moved on quickly 'Hasn't the blessing been with us when we did what The One said? Won't his blessing, his protection, be enough for us? Can't he do more for us than chariots?'

'So you're saying that The One has told us to go?' Jacob threw his hands up. 'I thought it was Abimelech! What if The One wants us to stay?'

'Stay and fight?' Rebecca's hands were on her hips. 'Outstay our welcome? Do you now want to make this our permanent home? You're crazy.'

'We'll see who's crazy,' grumbled Jacob. He knew that it was too late to change his father's decision.

As soon as they could gather their belongings, pay their bills, collect most of their debts, buy animals for transport, for meat and for their new skill of ploughing, Isaac led his company away from the city of Gerar. Esau spat at the city gates and proudly ran a running guard alongside his family's caravan. Jacob walked in the centre with Rebecca and Miriam, keeping an eye on the most precious stores.

In a couple of hours, they reached the part of the Gerar valley near the wells which grandfather Abraham had dug. He gave the order to make camp.

'So we're not going far away?' Jacob questioned Jeshach. 'is this a safe distance?'

'I recognise your understandable concern, sir, for the safety of our great company, a concern shared, I assure you, by your father.' Jeshach breathed deeply. 'You know that not everyone among the Philistines of Gerar was delighted to see us depart. Some have lost their employment or their trading partners. Some have developed genuinely affectionate relationships. Here we may benefit from their goodwill, well-deserved I must say, while at the same time honouring the agreement with King Abimelech and reacquainting ourselves with life without walls, with its challenges as well as its soul-freeing vistas.'

Jacob nodded slowly. As usual, listening to Jeshach's lengthy, confident, even, words drained his ability to sustain a challenge.

Beginning that afternoon Isaac had his father's wells enlarged, with a fresh wall. A team of young men led by Benjamin and Jeremiah, Miriam's nephews, spent days covering themselves in mud and sweat. Their muscles, unused to the confined angles of working inside a well, ached for a week.

Everyone gathered at the wells. 'When I was a young boy, I played by these wells. These wells proved the blessing of the One was with my father. These wells provided the blessing of water for him. These wells were blessed with the cooperation of the Philistines, with whom my father shared water. These wells were, for my father, Agreement and Harmony.

'We are here now in great number, far wealthier than we could have expected ten years ago. Our prosperity, and our return to these wells, show that the blessing of The One, the blessing of Abraham, is with us. These wells provide the blessing of water for us, and for our neighbours. We don't know how long we will remain here. The One will show us. In the meantime, remember the names: Agreement and Harmony. We seek agreement and harmony with our neighbours as my father did. Maybe now that there is some distance between us and the city of Gerar, we can look for renewed agreement, renewed harmony?'

'The old wells are now our wells. The old well-names are now again our well-names.' Isaac stood by one well and raised his staff over it. 'This well is Agreement!' He moved to the adjacent well. 'This well is Harmony. What are their names?'

'Agreement and Harmony' the company responded.

'What are their names?' asked Isaac more urgently.

'Agreement and Harmony!' came the more urgent reply.

'What are their names?' shouted Isaac, cajoling.

'Agreement and Harmony!' The voices rang out as one and arms were raised in celebration.

Apart from children who did not remember life away from a city, Isaac's company picked up the routines of walking a little further to collect firewood, of adjusting tent ropes in a new location, of enjoying fresher smells, resiny bushes instead of unemptied latrines, and seeing fewer strangers.

Isaac kept the animals grazing in the valley which they were used to. He selected some land to be ploughed, not far from the wells, so that barley and beans could be watered by hand, if necessary. Gerar city was not far away and trading continued, though not with everyone.

After a year, Isaac showed Ben and Jerry and team the spot he judged good to try for a fresh well nearer the animals.

Digging in fresh soil was even harder. A metre or so down they had to prise out large stones, before bashing through hard clay. But the clay soon became soft, their hopes rose, and they broke through to a bubbling underground spring. The hard work was rewarded. The blessing was seen to be still with Isaac. Questioning subsided.

One evening. just before Isaac's family ate, Jacob saw Ben and Jerry tearing through the camp, panting, half stumbling. They charged in, red-faced.

'Bastards! They're out to get us,' exclaimed Ben.

'They've claimed our well,' came the cooler voice of Jerry.

'Days it took, hard graft.'

'They say we're stealing their water.'

'They never even used to use this area.'

'They don't own the water!'

'They marched in and started harassing us.'

'What have we ever done to them?'

'What do you want us to do?'

Both young men stood, chests heaving still from their hurried journey, looking at Isaac.

'What to do? Mmm…,' mused Isaac. 'Have something to eat!' He smiled and beckoned them into the fore-tent to wash their hands and wait for the stretchable dinner.

Over marinaded chicken cooked with almonds and apricots, accompanied by piles of fresh flat bread, Ben and Jerry explained more detail. Three horsemen had ridden in, long swords hanging obviously on the horses' flanks.

They had camped close to the new well. They seemed friendly, though their comments about the local water being just what their Philistine horses needed were, in hindsight, beginning to assert their rights over the wells. Esau asked for more detail about the dress of the horses and riders and then nodded in sullen recognition.

The following day a dozen men came with sheep and goats, though only about a couple of dozen animals. They too set up camp. Isaac's men shared some bread and almonds with them and showed them how best to draw water. The Philistines in turn offered salt fish and wine, and then laughed pointedly at how afraid Isaac's men were of the sea and all its produce. The following day more Philistines arrived, then more. Before Isaac's men knew, they were outnumbered, shoved away from their well, accused of stealing Philistine water.

The Philistines made it plain that Isaac's people should leg it for their 'poxy hills' which they kept crowing about. That's where thieves and vagabonds go, land which no-one else wants. 'You've had more than your fair share of our water.'

The pair's bodies were now slumped with exhaustion. Their voices were fierce.

'We can teach them,' insisted Ben. 'They'll be too afraid to try anything like this again!'

'What do you want us to do?' repeated Jerry.

Isaac nodded slowly. 'So, some of them have taken against us.' His nodding was almost a rocking of the top half of his body. 'Yes...' He looked with compassion at the two young messengers. 'Thank you. You must be so tired! The One will show us, in the clearer light of day.'

Jacob searched for his father before breakfast. He found Isaac in one of the smaller store tents, in the cool, sitting on a sack of beans. The whites of his large eyes stood out in the half light. His forehead was scrunched.

'What's the battle plan?' Jacob was eager to right the wrong.

'I can't see it. I can't see it.' Isaac shook his head slowly. 'All I can see is more strife, more arguments, people injured. When will it end?'

'Hit them hard. Teach them a lesson. Make them afraid so that's the end of it.' Jacob's voice wasn't as strong as sure as his words.

Isaac raised his eyebrows and stared, wide-eyed, at his son. He sighed and shook his head. 'So, we're all warriors now? Is that how you want us to live? Become Ishmaelites?'

Jacob was taken aback by the suggestion that he was thinking like his father's angry dispossessed and dispossessing half-brother. 'Of course not. We're different. But we're not push-overs.'

'There are many ways of showing strength. Hitting back isn't the only one.' Isaac gave Jacob a serious stare. 'Sometimes it takes more guts to walk away.'

'Walk away!' Jacob was more annoyed with his father than he had ever been. 'Just slink away as though nothing's happened? Like frightened rabbits?'

'Slinking rabbits, that's new.' Isaac forced a chuckle. 'Look!' Isaac stood up, his eyes at the level of Jacob's chin.' If we walk away, we walk with our heads high, naming and shaming. They will know they're in the wrong, and we are choosing to let them off, this time.'

Jacob looked down at his father, uncomfortably close. He was puzzled and afraid and struggling to find words.

Isaac continued his challenge. 'We also walk away trusting. Haven't you heard it before? The One will provide! Whose well is it anyway?'

'We dug it. They did nothing.' Jacob was not so belligerent.

'Do the workmen own the building?' Isaac was now calmer, more like a teacher than an army officer. 'Or is it the owner of the land, the owner of the water, the one who instructs where to dig?'

Jacob was not ready to agree, nor continue fighting.

Isaac slapped his son on his shoulder. 'Time for breakfast. Come on.'

Isaac sent Jeshach with Ben and Jerry to find out who were the leaders of the Gerar herdsmen and set up a meeting with them. The meeting had to be on Isaac's terms, before they had time to plan, that morning, in the heat, not the usual cooler calmer evening. Isaac gathered 50 strong men and set off at the head of the contingent, with Esau and Jacob alongside him. As they marched down to the valley floor, they were visible to the Philistines.

A few large stones had been set up near the well, under a tree. Isaac and Jeshach, Esau and Jacob, sat at one side, with Ben and Jerry heading up the sombre 50 standing together behind them. Four Philistine leaders sat opposite, with a hastily assembled bunch of about 30 disorganised men behind them.

Jeshach stood up. 'We have a dispute and we are here to resolve it.' Jeshach's unusually loud, high-pitched, voice carried over the tense air. 'This is a dispute which you began, and which you are pursuing. Please be so kind… ' a forced smile on Jeshach's lips, 'as to explain the grounds for your contentious assertions and behaviour.'

The chief, or spokesman, stood up, looking about, as though hoping for a negotiator to come from the city. Hesitant at first, his words flowed more as he continued. 'We have lived in this valley for generations. Our great grandfathers' grandfathers led their herds here. This grazing was their grazing, preserved and handed to our generation. Our animals have been fed and watered here for more moons than there are leaves on this tree.'

'Yes, yes,' sighed Jeshach as though to himself but just loud enough for the speaker to hear. 'You've made your point.'

'When we see a poor, thin, family coming our way, we do not bar our gates and our hearts against them. We welcome the stranger, including the poor stranger, and we nurture them, as hens gathering under her feathers chicks orphaned by an unknown disaster. Our nurturing proves successful. The newly arrived birds put on much weight, they become strong and they multiply. We recognise that the time has come for them to leave our nest. They are many now, too many for us. They are strong now, too strong for us.'

Jeshach turned to Jacob next to him. 'I wonder who told them to say that?'

'These people now need a land of their own, with grazing of their own, and water of their own. This land, this grazing, this water, is not their own. May our ancestors forgive us if we give up the inheritance, the grazing, the water, which they passed to us!' The last word rang out as a rallying call to the people on his side, while the Philistine flung his arm towards the well. The Philistines nodded and stamped their feet in approval, their heads now up.

Jeshach nodded his head in recognition of a good attempt at a speech. He stood and cleared his throat. 'The water in this well of ours, as I am sure you know by now, is a fresh spring. Water from this new well will not deplete...' Isaac held up his hand. Jeshach fell silent as Isaac stood.

Isaac stretched and waved his right hand. 'Who can decide who made or owns the air? Who can decide who made or owns the land? Who can decide who made or owns the water under the land?' Isaac paused, looking around him. 'We can only decide what we know, from times we can remember. You remember this land as unbroken land. Your ancestors knew this land as unbroken land. We remember digging in this land. We remember the sweat and aching limbs. We remember the joyous blessing of finding a fresh, new, spring of water. We remember making this well.'

Isaac's men were now stamping in approval, heads held high.

'You say the water is yours. Who knows? We say, and you know, the well is ours.' This last word rang out loud in the defiant air.

'We say that the water can be shared. You have shared with us water from your wells. We were looking forward to sharing with you water from our well, as my father did.' Isaac's voice was now tender, fatherly.

'You have chosen not to share, but to make strife over this well, this water. You could have continued to water your flocks exactly as your ancestors did, with an extra shared supply. Instead, you wanted contention.' Isaac stared hard at the Philistine leaders and their supporters.

'As the digger of this well, I use my right to name this well. From now it is called "Strife." It is a well of strife and will have a history of strife. Meant to be a shared blessing, it will bear the curse of contention. I see many injuries being inflicted because of this well.' Jacob could sense that the men behind him were quieter, puzzled.

'You want strife?' called out Isaac. 'You can have it!' His men began to sound more ready for a fight.

'This well is Strife. You can have it. Here is your Strife.' Isaac went over to the Philistine leaders and led them to the well. He had the four of them stand around it and place their hands on the well wall.

'You have demanded strife and we give your Strife. We choose blessing over strife. We have One God whose blessing is strong enough for everyone. The One will provide. We can rely on him!' Isaac turned, sweeping his robe behind him. He put his arms round his sons' shoulders and shepherded them through their companions, away from the bemused Philistines.

Abraham's old wells had to be enough. Queues for water grew long. The mess made by hooves and droppings was not universally welcomed. Some people argued that domestic use should have priority over livestock, for what harm was there in animals having to wait a little longer? The herdsmen countered that it wasn't only the animals that were kept waiting. They had further to walk to take the animals to their pastures and so they should have priority. 'If we had fought for our other well, we wouldn't be in this mess,' was a common grumble. The well names seemed the opposite to the atmosphere around them. Was Isaac too soft? Might his son make a better leader? The strong and confident hunter? No-one thought of the little Mummy's boy as leader.

Livestock kept increasing. The following year even more healthy twins, and several triplets, were born. Isaac knew they needed another well. He toured the area again and again selected a spot for digging. This place was less open, tucked behind a little ridge, not the lowest point in that area, not the most likely for them to strike water.

The digging was harder too. More rock, some of which had to be slowly smashed. Ben, Jerry and their men took it in turns to drop into the dark shaft, pounding the floor underneath them, four, six, eight feet below the surface. Scratches and gashes from the jagged sides were common. Two men, distracted, pounded their own toes, making them hobblers for life. Once the rope hauling up the bucket of smashed rock snapped at the top and the floor went red with the blood from the diggers back. If only they had fought for their other well!

Jerry was nearly ten feet down, arms, legs, back aching again. He raised his spike and attacked the floor again, and again and again. He stumbled over the chippings and fell back against the rough wall. He took a deep breath and flexed himself again. He raised his spike and attacked with venom. His spike sank deep. His hands were suddenly two feet lower than they had ever been, tipping his body forward. Jerry jerked his head back from hitting the wall. His spike stood by itself, held in the rock. Jerry pulled it back up slowly. It came out with less effort than he expected, leaving a hole. Crouching, squashing himself to the ground, Jerry could see nothing in the hole. But could he, could he, smell water? He found a tiny pebble and dropped it through the hole. Did he, did he, hear a little 'tink' as it hit water?

With ingenious rope harnesses, each of the eager men took their turn in breaking the floor of the well through to a dark, cool, cistern which seemed to have been waiting for them.

'This is our well and our water!' Ben urged all who came to the well, at first to see, then to draw water. 'And we can defend this one.' The little ridge didn't make a fortress but they could see bandits coming from the South West.

'For now.' Jerry was the only one who dared temper Ben's belligerence. 'We may be moving on before long. This isn't really home, is it?'

The new well eased life for everyone. Most of the flocks watered there, leaving Agreement and Harmony for humans. The animals thrived. A few people, who said they had discerning palates, paid extra for the new water. In a few weeks they reported better digestion and deeper sleep when drinking water from the rock well.

Ben was planning a stockade around the new well. 'We won't give this up without a fight.' 'Have you asked Isaac?' Jerry knew the answer was no.

Esau heard about the planned stockade and was livid. 'The last thing we need! Show them we're expecting them to attack. Invite them! Let alone the mess from goats with nowhere to go. Attack is the best form of defence. Hit them hard, soon. Hit hard and move on smart.'

Esau set himself and his friends as the guardians of the new well. They reminded herdsmen. and especially the premium water sellers, how much this supply needed protection from the treacherous Philistines. 'Only yesterday a couple of them tried it on. We cleared them off back to their Strife water. It's a good thing we're here.' They didn't demand anything but they became very well-supplied, to coin a phrase, with everything they needed for their vital role.

Jacob made a mental calculation of what he saw Esau's men received in a couple of hours, not at the busiest time of day. He told his mother that they seemed to have the income of a very wealthy merchant's family. 'O yes,' Rebecca nodded, breathing out hard. 'He's been told and he forgets. He sees and he doesn't see. He knows and he doesn't know.'

One dinner Esau turned to his father. 'About time that new well had a name. Rock well. That's what they say. What's wrong with that?'

'Aah. I see,' replied Isaac softly. 'I see who thinks it's their well.' He paused for the memory of himself choosing that spot to resurface. 'I see disagreement. Maybe I see a fissure, splitting... I need to see more first.'

Life carried on. More twin sheep and goats were born. More barley grew strong. Esau's protectors clung to their easy role. Jacob dropped enough comments about how much they ate and slept to rile enough people to make Esau know that he was not universally popular. Esau was not bothered. He seemed to relish being seen as something of a bandit himself. Competition grew between the, now several, premium water sellers, some drawing by day, some by night. Water jars sprang surprising leaks. Donkeys became surprisingly lethargic. Isaac knew and he didn't know, he saw and he didn't see. He kept quiet.

Another good harvest needed all available labour. As usual, the beginning of harvest coincided with the most auspicious time for Esau's main hunting expedition. Jacob knew Esau couldn't demean himself by swinging a silly shaped knife at a prey which stood perfectly still, rooted to the ground.

The guard, (or was it an excuse for an easy life for bullies?) was down to two sixteen-year-olds. Four Philistine herds converged from different directions. The guards ran at the small herd approaching from the South West. The other herds simply walked in and made themselves at home. They now commanded the ridge.

'Breakfast is waiting for you.' Rebecca stood in front of Jacob, her loud words dragging him out of sleep.

Jacob squinted. 'The sun...? It's too early!' Only the

first light of dawn came through the tent opening which Rebecca had flung back.

'A decision has to be made. Don't you remember?' snapped Rebecca. 'If we have to be up early for making breakfast, why should you lie in when you have work to do?' This wasn't the first time Jacob's mother had made a sharp comment about decisions being man's work.

Jacob wanted to be involved in this decision. After what felt like years of holding back and saying hardly anything when his father, brother and the leading men were consulting, he had managed to say a few words which had been received well enough. He still had to push himself to open his mouth but now the pushing was from one firm inner arm rather than two desperate ones. Without Esau, he felt more free to talk. This robbery of their God-given well had to be resisted. The Philistines, and everyone else, needed to know that this family could hold their ground, their well.

Jacob was beginning to enjoy thinking of his future leadership, unlikely though it appeared. Esau, with his brash bravado, was still the one people flattered with talk of how well he would step into his father's shoes. He couldn't see that Esau would even want him as a senior advisor. Esau had never paid attention to Jacob's views. Their mother, of course, saw their future differently. Far from dismissing his growing interest in decision making for good and ill, she encouraged it.

'How do we take back control of our well? That's what we here for, right?' Ben strode into the tent looking around. Jerry followed him, saying nothing. Jeshach and Amos were standing at the back of the tent, Jacob nearer the opening.

'Good to have you with us, Ben, and Jerry,' welcomed Jacob. 'They shouldn't get away with it again!'

'Too right!' spat out Ben.

'Everyone's mad about it,' added Jerry, 'more than last time.'

'How good of you to come and assist us, Benjamin, Jeremiah.' Jeshach had moved to greet the younger men and now nodded to each with a broad smile. 'The situation in which we find ourselves is grave indeed and needs careful consideration indeed. What will be the best course of action is not always abundantly clear, and, as so often, what is decided today may well have a significant bearing on the whole course of our future.'

'Jeshach!' remonstrated Jacob with a swift wink towards Ben. 'You don't have to make everything complicated! Or be cautious about everything!'

'No, sir.' Jeshach raised his eyebrows. 'Your contribution is much appreciated, sir. Our discussions will cover every approach to…'

'Have you begun already?' called Rebecca as she entered the tent just behind Isaac and in front of a servant carrying a tray with mint tea and honey. Isaac, in a dark grey robe, walked slowly. He fixed each person briefly with his large eyes and sat on his cushioned seat.

'Do you want to carry on without the head of the family?' challenged Rebecca. 'Tea! That always helps. Then you can make a fresh start.' She motioned to the servant to put the tea on the small table in the middle of the tent, covered with a faded red and purple cloth. The others sat on stools and accepted their tea. Isaac now looked like the head. Standing, Isaac was a little shorter than Jacob, but dwarfed by portly Jeshach, wiry Amos, muscular Ben and Jerry.

'Rebecca, my love, do you have urgent work to do?' asked Isaac.

Rebecca raised her eyebrows at her husband.

'We might need you to fetch more tea at a crucial moment,' Isaac chuckled. 'and keep us sweet!'

Rebecca pulled the double curtain in front of the tent opening and sat next to it, a little away from the men, smoothing the folds on her grey working robe.

'Time to be serious,' said Isaac. 'Jeshach, please will you set the scene for us?'

'The question before us,' Jeshach looked particularly at Ben, 'is how we respond to the unprovoked and extremely serious aggression of some elements among our erstwhile hosts and friends? I think we all agree that their behaviour is completely unwarranted and damaging to the wellbeing of our entire community?' Nods, grunts, 'Yes,' 'Of course.'

'Before we address in detail what shall be our response, it is good, as a preliminary, to remind ourselves of our respective roles here. Benjamin, Jeremiah, without your key role, your sterling work, we may well not have had this problem today. You are known and respected in our community for your labour and also for your continuing commitment to the prosperity of us all. Unlike some among us, you have not sought personal gain but have rightly seen your prosperity as allied to the general prosperity of our entire company. You have been brought into this council because your views, your passions, your voices, are highly valued. We want the whole community to know that you have been fully able to express your point of view on this matter. We encourage you, though I don't think you need much encouragement, to express yourselves fully and forthrightly, with the respect that I know you have for the family head.

'You know that my role is Advisor. I bring my experience and a limited detachment to all questions about which our head has a decision to make. I am well used to having my advice questioned, even disregarded and have, at times, been eventually grateful that courses of action which seemed to me, at the time, to be obvious and necessary, were not followed, whereas the courses which I deemed risky or imprudent proved to be more beneficial, more blessed, than I could have expected.

Amos has a similar advisory role. Amos brings a similar limited detachment, together with a remarkable intuitive grasp of the essence of a matter, an ability to envisage an outcome, and an unpredictable sense of, to be straightforward, the contribution The One wants to make. I have learned that the seriousness with which our head receives, and weighs, the distinctive contributions of Amos is justified.

Jeremiah and Benjamin, for today you join us as advisors. All of us recognise that it is our head who solely bears the responsibility of the decision. It will be forever known as his decision. Even if he were to retire and say nothing, leaving others to take the lead, the responsibility for this abdication would be entirely his. Our presence together proves that such is not the case today. Our head will make a decision, fully advised by each of us in our own way.

'Having known and willingly served our head for many years, I am certain that Isaac will not only listen to us, but also to the voice, the intimations, the indications, of The One. Who is the best, the most far-seeing, advisor? Can any of us claim such a role? There is One who all, on reflection, recognise as the truly wonderful counsellor. We put our trust in His ability to continue to guide and bless our company.'

Rebecca nodded with her head and shoulders while the men looked more or less blank. She smiled at Jacob. Jacob had noticed that his role had not been specified. Was he not an advisor too? Only an observer? Or maybe, his mother would say, a future head?

'Thank you, Jeshach.' Isaac had a restrained smile for Jacob. 'We all know what has happened and there is no good to come of talking about why it happened. The question indeed is 'What do we do now? How do we respond?' I will be interested to hear your views on this question.' He looked round at all five men and settled on Amos. 'Trusted prophet, what has come to you?'

'Slavery! I see us as slaves, God forbid! But I can see it.' Amos held his head high, his face both bright and sad. 'Trust in The One. Trust in the One. That's what I hear. Early in the morning. Trust in The One who never fails to make the sun rise!'

Isaac looked down, keeping silence. Ben shuffled.

'Tireless worker,' Isaac looked at Ben, 'what do you see as the best way forward.'

'Not being slaves to them! Fighting them as their equals and betters. They steal the water that keeps us alive. They want us dead, they want to drive us out, they want to do away with us. Now is the time to fight for the right to live and to live here!' Ben looked round challenging disagreement.

Jeshach looked ready to take up the challenge but Isaac motioned to him to sit back. 'Man of strong arms and strong heart,' Isaac looked intently at Jerry, eyes even wider, 'what seems best to you?'

'It was The One who led us to the water, through you, sir,' Jerry's voice was calm. 'The water gives us the freedom to live here, without the water we'd be as good as dead. He must want us to keep the water, the well, not them. He'll be with us as we take it back.'

Jacob nodded so all could see. Rebecca looked at him as though surprised.

'I want you to know, Benjamin and Jeremiah, how much your work for our community, your commitment to our well-being, is appreciated.' Isaac spoke with fatherly gentleness. 'You are great young men of whom we are very proud.'

'Thank you, sir,' said Jerry. Ben looked with suspicion.

'Hmmmm…' Isaac breathed deeply. He shut his eyes. Jacob thought he was maybe uncomfortable with being the smallest man in the room. 'Trust in the One! How do we do that? What does that mean for us now?'

Before anyone could break his silence, Isaac thrust his hand towards Ben and Jerry and almost shouted. 'You think it means we are to trust The One to give us victory over our well-stealing enemies. Yes, we can understand you.

My son and heir has much sympathy for your call to arms.'
He smiled at Jacob assuring him that he did not mean his
absent brother. 'Trust in the One and fight. Fight and trust
in The One. Hmm. How will we know if victory comes
through our own strength? Amos! When you hear 'Trust in
the One' do you see us fighting? You only said you could see
us as slaves, God forbid!'

Isaac held up his right hand. 'You know what I have
thought up until now. Trust in The One to provide for us,
to give us water which we don't have to kill for. That felt
like risky trusting, unpopular trusting.' He challenged Ben,
Jerry and Jacob with his gentle eyes. 'Was I wrong?'

'The new well!' cut in Amos. 'The blessing remains!'

Jeshach nodded. Rebecca smiled.

'Slavery? What is slavery?' mused Isaac. 'Is it living
free through out-fighting our neighbours? Countering their
counter-attack, always needing to be stronger? Are we
Ishmaelites?'

Amos shook his head fiercely.

'Can we live more free than that?' Isaac stood up and
swept the faces with his eyes. 'Can we live by trusting only
in the blessing of The One? Can we live by not fighting? I
want us to keep trying!'

'Trust in The One!' acclaimed Amos.

Ben and Jerry stayed sitting. Jacob started to rise, ready
to challenge on their behalf. Surely it was time for him to
make his contribution. Rebecca frowned at him, jerking her
head down momentarily. Jacob slumped back in his seat,
put in his place again.

'Our new well is a sign of blessing, but it has brought

its problems.' Isaac calmly shook his head. 'Rivalries, jealousies, competition, even enmity. Is this a well which makes enemies?' Rebecca nodded.

'Painful though it is, especially to those who have invested their sweat, their bodies, their friends, in this well...' Isaac looked tenderly again at Ben and Jerry. 'Painful though it is, I see no reason to change now our way of trusting in The One. They already have the well 'Strife,' for all the good it will do to them! I name our new well "Enmity!" They are welcome to it. We will move on and trust in better. Thank you, gentlemen! And my beautiful companion.' Isaac smiled at Rebecca and went to hug each man in turn, beginning with Jacob.

Later that day Rebecca found Jacob sitting on an outcrop facing Enmity Well in the middle distance.

'Jake!' hailed Rebecca. 'Are you sore? Why dwell on it? Are you planning a heroic recapture?

Jacob turned away and snorted.

'OK! You don't want company!' His mother smiled. 'But you know I'll have my say sooner or later. Why put it off?

'Huh.'

'So... you were on the side of the hotheads and your father stood up to them.' Rebecca's voice was tender, friendly and firm.

'He didn't even let me speak!' Jacob snarled.

'Was he wrong when he said that you agreed with them?' Rebecca cajoled. 'Did he not acknowledge your view publicly? Did you want a confrontation?'

'He's ignored me for too long!'

'What good would it have done you to have a public rift with your father? Others can disagree with him, blow their tops and no one thinks of forming a break-away camp. Don't you see it's different with you?'

'Would that be so terrible?' Jacob rolled his eyes.

'Disastrous! You will have your time to lead, Jake, love. It'll come.'

'So now I have to put up with us slinking away again?' Jacob spat.

'So now you have to accept your father standing up to the hotheads. And when are there no hotheads? You remember this! Hotheads lead into trouble.'

'Let them walk over us then? Let them keep driving us away until there's no land for us?'

'You really think these Philistines can undo what The One has promised? There is reason to see them as almighty? There will be land for us, can't you wait for it?'

Jacob looked down and shook his head slowly. Rebecca waited.

Eventually Jacob stood up. 'All right, all right! We move on again. There's packing up to do.'

Rebecca hugged her son and they walked down to the camp together.

Isaac led his great company towards a trading outpost to replenish supplies. They camped nearby. Isaac called a feast. They were wealthy in livestock and grains and beans.

They could afford the best oil and wine, dried fruit and nuts, earthenware and leather goods. The aroma of roasted meat, the sound of raucous singing, the hope of one day having a more permanent home. Songs celebrated the great well diggers and honoured the great well chooser. The community felt again how much they shared in common.

Isaac invited a few merchants with whom he had traded happily for years, with their families. Jacob wondered how their people would feel about having Philistines at their feast. These merchants seemed to be regarded as decent men. The lavish gifts they brought helped soothe soreness. They praised the longsighted wisdom and generosity of Isaac and his people. Once again, comments were made about good and bad Philistines, as in every tribe and people.

'You would have thought they could see that your wells were not depriving them of water!' A particularly chubby Philistine dealer in wine and oil, wearing green robes, laughed as he spoke. 'These ignorant herdsmen with brains no bigger than a goat's!'

'A superstitious bunch,' agreed his compatriot, a leaner livestock dealer, in dark brown robes with thin black stripes. 'They have fixed ideas about where their gods will protect their animals. Only up to that hill and no further!'

'You'll have to tell me more,' invited Isaac. 'I've been wondering if there ever will be a place where they won't quarrel about us digging a well.'

The following day six traders came together to offer Isaac their commiserations and their advice. Isaac thanked them for their understanding and help. 'It's to our advantage!' smiled the chubby dealer. 'We want our grandchildren to be dealing with you too.'

The traders not only showed Isaac the rough boundary beyond which there would be less likelihood of contention, they also offered a couple of experienced workmen. Philistine knowledge of house and tower building could be of great use in building a well shaft. Ben and Jerry and colleagues again put their all into digging at the spot which Isaac chose. All the fit men took turns to assist, carrying away earth and stones, bringing larger building stones. The cooperation, experience and fresh expertise meant that no-one was injured.

The new well was further from Gerar and the sea, closer to the hills. In this undulating land, almost foothills, the digging was harder. They hacked and excavated in hope, holding to themselves the 'What if we don't strike water?' The cheer when the bottom of the shaft started filling up from one side was loud and long.

'Friends!' shouted Isaac as all gathered at the new well. 'This is our best well ever! We have known the disappointment of wells stolen from us. We have wondered how The One could have allowed such robbery. We have mourned for lost hopes and wasted effort. We have wondered if we will ever have such a substantial well, with such clear water.

'The One had a better well in mind, here! He replaces what has been stolen from us with a stronger well which will last for generations. He leads us to water with the taste of the hills. He leads us to build in harmony.

'Maybe we should not have turned our backs on all our Philistine friends. Maybe we should have remembered the help freely given to help us to plough and to sow. Maybe we could have dug in cooperation earlier and enjoyed a more secure well sooner. We live and we learn...

'This well is our best well ever! When we felt hemmed in by people acting as enemies, we have been led to a land and a well where we have no threats, where we can come and go and share freely. Now The One has made room for us. Now the One has given us a place to be fruitful. This is our best well ever. This is The Open Spaces Well!'

As Isaac prompted, the people proclaimed the name of the new well. Digging in three different places and striking water each time was indeed a blessing to be celebrated.

At first Esau took up his role of Chief Guard of the Open Spaces well. Many agreed that they needed still to be on their guard. Isaac continued to stress that this was to be a well open to anyone in the area, a hospitable well. Over the next six months, Isaac's trader friends led their compatriots, including herdsmen, to draw occasionally from Open Spaces. Tension evaporated. Esau's guards grew bored and people started making comments in their presence about 'doing some real work for a change.' Isaac mentioned to Esau that good money was being offered for gazelle horns as well as for dried venison. (Everyone knew Isaac was partial to his venison.) 'A permanent hunting party is what we need!' exclaimed Esau. 'Get the wine ready!'

The hunting thrived, along with the rearing and sowing and reaping. The camp was half a day's journey from the main trading route, too far for them to be bothered by a stream of visitors and near enough for selling direct to passing Syrians and Egyptians. Jacob enjoyed the bargaining. Their hides, especially, fetched better prices than from the regular traders. Thankfully they had enough to satisfy both sets of customers.

Walking back up from the plain to their low slopes, raising eyes to the hills beyond, Jacob would smile with longing. Other people were very contented with Open Spaces. They had a good living, their tents stocked with tin plates and juicy raisins from across land and sea. Why move away up into the rough and remote ravines?

'What is about those hills?' asked Jacob to himself. The fresher air, the longer views, the safety of physical barriers to raiders and soldiers? The attachment of grandfather Abraham who had journeyed so far for these particular hills? Or simply the longing of home? Was his yearning the natural love of every man for the land on which he first set his baby eyes? Or was he pulled by the renewed call of The One? Yet hadn't The One said that this coastal land was now theirs as much as the original hills?

Esau often said that in the hills the game was better, the hunting more satisfying. Fellow feeling with his twin brother was a strange emotion for Jacob. He was also comforted by this element of companionship. More importantly, Jacob could see his father, from time to time, lift his large eyes to the hills too. Was this where the help, the blessing, of The One, would come most consistently?

After two years of Open Spaces, Jacob thought his father gazed more and sortied more away from the prosperous plain. After the next ample harvest had been celebrated and stored in a couple of fresh tents, Isaac announced the time had come to move on and up.

'The blessing has been with us here, indeed.' Isaac nodded his head at those he knew were particularly content with Open Spaces. He chuckled. 'Where can we go where The One cannot bless us? Where can we escape from his attention? You just try! When we moved down here 15 years ago, I never expected to stay this long. Did anyone?'

The older heads, particularly, shook in agreement.

'More seriously – for once!' continued Isaac, with an eye twinkling to Rebecca. 'I, for one, came down from the hills with a promise in my heart, and my head, to return. Promises have to be kept. The older I grow, the more important I see the keeping of promises.' Isaac looked steadily at the faces sitting before him.

'We go,' Isaac's voice rose loud, 'with our heads held high! No-one is forcing us out. We go with blessing. Who knows what wells await us up there? Who knows if The One will send us back down here before long? We return, as promised, and we'll see.' Isaac beamed.

Isaac's confidence dampened, though not extinguished, the muttering. This time they were being uprooted for no apparent reason. Why could they not stay in the 'Open Spaces' with their best well yet, which no-one wanted to steal from them? Had the Philistines actually put on pressure, made them unwelcome, again? Was Isaac too accommodating, moving on before the Philistines became aggressive? Why leave for an area less green?

Yet Isaac was their leader. No-one wanted to work for a Philistine. They trekked South and East, away from the sea, up into a more arid land.

CHAPTER FIVE

Settled

(Genesis 26:24-33)

A couple of days after they moved, without investigating the new area at all, Isaac gave instructions to dig a well. Digging just where they happened to be was a shot in the dark, according to some of the older men. Isaac also had an altar built, and started to make a permanent site for his tent. Everyone gathered at this altar and Isaac explained that he had been visited again.

'Don't be afraid! There really is nothing to fear. The blessing is still with us, especially here.' Isaac looked happy, smiling and excited. 'He came to me last night. I wish you could have seen him! The light around him has a music of its own.' Isaac hummed. 'To start with, it is the strangest thing you have ever seen. Then you realise that it is safe, the safest you have ever known. Just to be in that light...! And there he is, sitting on his heels completely relaxed. He looks as though he has everything under control and he makes you think that nothing could possibly go wrong. There he is as though that's where he always is. And he looks more human than any idol I've ever seen and brighter and more beautiful. I wish you could have seen him.'

Isaac's face had a kind of sheen that doesn't come with alcohol or anything else men might find to brighten them up. On that second night, with everyone still tired from the journey, and sentries posted around the new place just in case, there had been no feasting, no celebration that might attract unwanted attention.

'So, there he is looking and acting like a friend who's used to dropping in and feels quite at home and he says "I'm the God of your father Abraham." Well, you don't expect that, even if it isn't the first time. Just casually, "I'm God" like someone would say "I'm your cousin." At the time you just go along with it. It's only after that you realise how bizarre the conversation was. "I am with you." He stressed each word. Not great super-religious words, very ordinary words. "I... AM... WITH... YOU." And not fiercely like "Pay good attention to this or else!" Just with enough emphasis for you to know this is important and you probably couldn't forget it if you tried.'

'Then he carried on "I will bless you," It was like the sun coming out from behind a cloud when he said that. Like rainbows arching out from him in every direction. Like he wanted you to see the blessing, not just hear about it. "And I will make your offspring numerous, for the sake of Abraham, my servant." Well, I thought we were pretty numerous already. But there's more!'

'So, this is a good place, a really good place. The One

is with us here. You'll see what happens as we make this a home. I'm pretty sure we'll have an even better well so we can make this,' Isaac flung open his arms to indicate the land around, 'we can make this green! Come on, let's eat!'

Isaac wanted everyone to celebrate, to join in his joy. Fires were lit and animals were selected and slaughtered and people went to look at the well being dug and came back to find where they had packed their best clothes. And then another surprise. Isaac looked bemused as everyone stared to his left. He peered and questioned Esau. Dust in the distance: a company of travellers, an army even, heading towards them.

The atmosphere changed like a cold wind had suddenly buffeted everybody. Hadn't they left to move away from trouble, and here was trouble trying to find them! They didn't know whether to wear their party clothes or their battle clothes, whether to break out the supplies or hide them. 'Don't be afraid!' said Isaac, still smiling broadly. He walked round the camp shouting the instruction. 'It's fine for him to say it,' grumbled more than a few. 'Easier said than done.' 'Where did caution and common sense go?' They followed their leader, reassured that he had sent scouts out to find out who the visitors were and start negotiations, if needed. Most of the people, Jacob among them, had gathered for the feast when the Philistines arrived.

They were Philistine soldiers, some of the best, but in ceremonial, not battle, dress. Matching light grey cloaks, fringed with orange to match their vests. A couple of dozen on horseback, but not an army. Three chariots, no less. The army commander's black and rugged, the Prime Minister's finer, maroon with silver decoration, and the King's, golden, well upholstered, with four horses. Each carried their exalted owners. Some of them could remember having to jump back smartly whenever these charged through the streets or the market in Gerar. It seemed strange to see the same chariots enter their camp at a steady walk, following the escort sent to meet them.

Isaac called Esau and Jacob to join him. They stood behind Isaac while Jeshach and the other servants-in-chief stood next to him. It was a scene which stayed vivid in Jacob's memory.

'Greetings, King of the Philistines,' said Isaac cheerily. He stopped, waiting. He was not ready for an elaborate speech of welcome. The purpose of the visit needed to be made known first.

'Greetings, Isaac the blessed!' proclaimed the Abimelech. He also stopped there. He seemed to think that it was not his place to dictate the conversation. Tension mounted as the leaders eyeballed each other, waiting for the other to make the first move. Afterwards Jacob could see how the King holding back, even deferring to his father, was a good sign. At the time, it made people wonder how quickly they could lay hands on their swords.

'You have come to find me?' Isaac laughed a little. 'Why? You don't want anything to do with me, you hate me, you sent me away from you?' Isaac's arm gestures were a little exaggerated. He seemed to find it all a great joke. Or wanted to give that impression to soften his sharp words.

'We can see, Isaac. We have eyes and we use them well.' said the King, opening his arms to include the officers with him. 'We have seen you grow and prosper. We have seen your flocks and your servants increase. We have seen an invisible hand guiding you, protecting you. We have seen that your God, your One, has been with you.' Jacob could hardly believe his ears. If anyone doubted what his father had said about God being with them, they now had it confirmed the same day by no-one less than the Philistine King! Had their God been able to arrange this visit, this declaration? What about all the Philistine gods? Did they just have to do the One's bidding?

Isaac nodded heartily and laughed a more relaxed laugh. 'Is it that obvious?' he said to those close to him.

The King continued. 'We have met in council and would like to put a proposal to you, Isaac the blessed. I think you know Ahuzzath my Chief Advisor, and General Phicol, Commander in Chief?' He motioned to Ahuzzath.

'If I may follow up these astute words?' said the Prime Minister to Isaac. Jacob had not expected Ahuzzath to be asking his father's permission to speak, not after being invited to speak by his own king. Isaac said cheerily 'Of course!'

'We have reflected together on what our esteemed King has observed, and we can see that it is only right that we should honour both his wise observation and the substance of his remarkably clear sight.' Jacob recognised the oily style of diplomat-speak so fond to Jeshach. 'We concur that you have become a highly significant factor in our regional relations, and that this is, no doubt, due to a power higher than ours.' Here the Minister nodded to the King. 'Recognising your position and looking for your prosperity to continue to increase, we would like to serve you in any way that we can. We see that there are mutual benefits to be gained by cooperation and we would not want these benefits to be diminished, or, heaven forbid, removed, through any unfortunate little quarrels taking on an importance which they certainly do not warrant, given the long-term mutual flourishing to which we, and we trust, you too, aspire.' Jeshach nodded from his chest with deep sagacity. He was in his element. Jacob didn't know whether to admire their Steward for being in the same league as the Philistine Prime Minister or to mistrust him for it.

'In short, we consider that the time is propitious for us to bind ourselves to you with bonds of esteem and friendship. We would like to offer you an alliance, the terms of which to be agreed mutually, but to include such mechanisms as will be mutually beneficial towards the resolving of disputes of a minor and local nature, so that they do not impair the continuing high regard and future partnership one for the other.' He didn't mention wells as such but everyone knew the history. He gracefully retired a step or two.

Phicol cleared his throat. 'We are of one mind.' He nodded formally to his fellow visitors. Jacob wondered why they needed to stress how much they agreed. Were they hiding unspoken tensions? 'We envisage peace through mutual strength. You will not harm us, just as we have done you no harm.' He paused and looked boldly at Isaac. 'We have done nothing to you but good. We enabled you to move on in peace into your chosen territory.' He bowed stiffly and stepped back. Jacob could think of several ways in which this account of their history had, to say the least, been brightly polished.

The King smiled broadly. 'You are blessed by your God, Isaac. Now you are blessed. Please welcome the blessing which we have recognised.' Jacob wondered what he meant by the blessing 'now.' Was he implying that their offer of an alliance was the greatest blessing and woe betide them if they refused it?

Isaac didn't seem to have any doubts. 'Welcome indeed! Such good news! You know, you had us puzzled, worried even, coming here with such an escort. Thank you for your unexpected and welcome offer of an alliance. It sounds a good plan. But we can't negotiate as strangers. Come and eat, come and tell us some of your famous stories. We'll work out the detail in the morning.'

Abimelech was clearly the most keen to enjoy the meat, the wine (originally from Philistine traders) and the company. He laughed with Isaac, enjoying his company again. Maybe he had few others with whom he could relax in the same way? Ahuzzah and Phicol loosened up as well. In the morning the negotiations did not take long. The Philistines even accepted a specific clause about shared water rights, with the priority for the well-digger. Oaths were exchanged. The alliance was forged.

From his chariot the King led the farewells. 'Peace be with you Isaac the blessed! Whatever happens on the roads ahead of us, we will always be friends. We will live in peace.' 'Peace be with you, Abimelech!' returned Isaac. 'May there always be peace between us.'

Back in their tent, Rebecca rustled up the finest meal possible. They talked of how tentative Abimelech had been, of Ahuzzah greasy as ever, of Phicol grumping out his words as though a sword was pricking his back. They drank and reminisced and laughed.

'Well!' Isaac chuckled again, his hands resting on his full belly. 'If that isn't The One's doing, I don't know what is! What did we do to achieve an alliance with such favourable terms? Did we defeat their army? Did we hold a store city to ransom? I don't think we did anything, except move away in peace. What a blessing!' He shook his head in wonder.

'And a curse?' Rebecca looked down with a coy smile. She knew she was setting a riddle.

'A curse to be partnered with those slippery seafarers from now on?' questioned Esau. 'Maybe!'

Isaac shook his head. 'I think my beloved may have been thinking about the past rather than the future?' His eyebrows raised as he looked at Rebecca. She glanced up at Isaac and smiled.

'Mum! What are you thinking now?' pleaded Jacob.

'What did we do to achieve this alliance?' Rebecca looked round, waiting for her question to sink in. 'Did we give them Strife and Enmity? Do they now live with Strife and Enmity?'

Jacob frowned at the memory of the thefts. Esau spoke to his left shoulder but loud enough to be heard. 'We can't go on just giving everything away.'

'I wonder what strife and enmity Abimelech is now

having to resolve?' Rebecca held her head up, her eyes piercing her sons. 'Have they started killing each other? Or just shouting at each other and stealing from each other?'

Isaac nodded. 'Could well be, my love!' He smiled at her. 'Gaining something the wrong way may well bring a curse rather than a blessing. There's something else for you to remember, lads.' Jacob thought his father seemed to be looking at him more than his brother. Another odd gesture Jacob was not going to stress about.

'We've found water!' The well diggers came running through the camp. 'It's almost gushing!' 'Worth seven of their wells.' Isaac laughed again. 'The well of the oath! Seven times blessed!' he declared, 'Beer-Sheba.' This was the place to be, to settle. Soon there would be houses rather than tents.

A few days later Jacob was called into his father's tent, into the meeting area with colourful carpet and cushions. Esau arrived at the same time, looking puzzled at and threatening to his little brother. Isaac welcomed them both and gestured for them to sit on cushions next to him. Esau quickly sat closest to his father, looking at home. He shifted his cushion a little, away from Jacob. Jacob felt uncomfortable, still not used to such familiarity with his father. But he was not going to let Esau snub him. He moved his cushion closer as well.

'I can't stop thinking about Abimelech's visit. I just want you to remember it and see how amazing it was.' Isaac looked at his sons, who nodded.

'Remember this meeting. Remember how it all

happened. Keep them to the agreement. No more nonsense about wells! And make sure our people honour it too. We have some hotheads too, you know! You have to restrain them. That's what we're here for, why we make the decisions in the end.'

So far it was Isaac who had made the decisions. Was Jacob now included as a decision-maker?

'Of course, the hotheads will always find a reason for having a go. They love a fight, especially one that looks pretty easy and makes them into heroes. Hold them back. Stop them from making things worse. It's not worth it. In the long run it doesn't pay.'

Isaac looked sternly at Esau. Esau smiled and nodded in a relaxed way. When Isaac carried on speaking, Esau let his eyes wander to the doorway.

'Mostly, boys, relax!' Isaac continued. 'It's not up to us. It really isn't. God told me he would bless me, and you as well, my offspring, for the sake of your grandfather. You each have your own blessing. We don't have to do anything special. He'll do what he's already promised. We just make sure our plans don't get in his way!'

'You remember that I once thought seriously of moving on to Egypt?' Jacob and Esau nodded. 'Temporary, at first at least. You can't always rely on the rain in this land. Not like in Egypt with their enormous river. But HE' Isaac pointed up, 'HE said "Don't go there! Don't go to Egypt." "OK!!" I said. "If that's what you want, though an explanation would be nice." '

Isaac chuckled and shook his head. 'I know you remember the wells. You know the first step, the important one? He said "Don't go" and I didn't. And now here we are, better off than I could have imagined. Going to Egypt would have been my plan getting in the way of his plan.' Isaac spoke more softly and seriously. 'Don't let your plan get in the way of HIS plan. OK lads?'

'Yes, Dad,' Jacob said quickly. He enjoyed being included in this man talk, the kind of conversation Isaac and Esau used to share between themselves. His father's arm round his shoulder still felt odd.

'Yeah, but we have to plan,' said Esau, annoyed, loud. 'And we have to take the chances when they come!'

Isaac took Esau's rudeness in his stride. 'Whose plan do you think is best?'

'We've been given eyes. We can remember how things work out. We're not meant to sit on our arses waiting for an angel to drop out of the sky!' Jacob looked aghast at his father, letting him know he did not approve of Esau's manner.

Isaac chuckled gently. 'How far can your eyes see? Into tomorrow? Not even beyond lunchtime! I could see the land dried up, cracked. I could imagine the great river. It seemed obvious. All this,' Isaac stretched his arm in an arc to his right, 'I couldn't see. But He could.' Isaac paused. 'OK. Most of the time we can just carry on sorting things out ourselves. But if you think He might be trying to tell you something, pay attention!'

Esau grunted.

'And do you know what the hardest thing to do is?' pressed Isaac.

'No, father,' said Jacob quickly with as much respect as he could put into two words.

'But you're going to tell us,' drawled Esau.

'Nothing!' Isaac's chuckle this time was louder and longer. 'Doing nothing can be really hard. If we weren't going to Egypt, what were we to do? Nothing. He had it in hand. We just had to sit still and wait.'

'Yes, Father I can see that,' said Jacob keenly.

'Well,' challenged Esau, 'what works one day can be a disaster the next! Thanks for your advice, Dad. But today's a cooler day and the animals are more likely to be out. We need some meat. I don't want to waste time.'

'Enjoy the hunting!' said Isaac, still not angry. 'And think about what I've said.'

'Yeah, Dad,' said Esau dismissively. He walked out.

Isaac smiled at Jacob. 'I really will remember what you've said,' Jacob said awkwardly.

Isaac nodded. 'Good.' There was a strained silence.

'I think it's time to check on the hens,' said Jacob.

Isaac looked at him a little wistfully. 'OK!' he said cheerily. Jacob left, wondering what all that had been about.

'Judith, Basemath, do you want anything from the big market?' Rebecca called into the large new tent topped with small blue and black flags. Jacob saw the fluttering scraps of cloths and wondered again what kind of gods would be pleased to see such rubbish.

'Hello…! Judith, Basemath!' Rebecca's voice was gentle, friendly. 'We're on our way and thought you might like us to bring you something.'

A deep lingering grunt, not unlike a cow slowly letting

out wind, came through the tent wall. Then words in the same tone. 'Minute. Just minute'

More than five minutes later, a woman's head came through the loosely tied tent door. Luxuriant brown hair was piled like a half-made bird's nest on her head, one rogue wave flopping over her right eye. Her large brown left eye fought against the early morning light. 'What?' The languid head moved side to side. 'What time? He back?'

'Good morning, Judith,' breezed Rebecca. 'It's time for us to go to the market. We thought you might like something. Esau's not back yet.'

'Uh!' The head was sucked back into the tent. The sound of a slap and a cry, a jumble of sleepy voices, grunts, whispering, made Jacob and Rebecca raise their eyebrows to each other.

Eventually, the woman's head emerged again, eyes blinking. The high-itched voice was stern. 'You remember?'

'Yes, Judith.' Rebecca tried not to sigh. 'We will remember what you would like. But not everything may be available this week. There is no guarantee that your particular products will be in stock.' Jacob knew the previous complaints about orders not being fulfilled.

The head frowned, either because she didn't like the words or didn't understand them. 'OK! We need. You ready?'

'Yes indeed,' Rebecca's voice was prompt and eager.

'Rose oil, large jar.' Rebecca couldn't help raise her eyebrows again. Rose scent was more subtle than their previous choices. 'Cassia oil, large jar.' Judith looked at Rebecca until Rebecca nodded. Then Judith relaxed into a sly smile. 'Salt fish. 3 packets '

Jacob was not alone in hating the fishy smell and the Hittite women knew it.

'You wait!' The head withdrew, the audience placed on pause.

Three long minutes later, the bottom of the tent door was opened and a water jar was pushed forward by two many-bangled hands. Judith shouted from inside. 'You get bring water now!'

'And from which well would you like your water today? And which particular servant…' challenged Jacob.

'Shh!' interrupted Rebecca. She stood tall. 'I'm terribly sorry, but all our servants are occupied at the moment. When you're dressed, maybe you could go and ask someone politely to help you out. You must have hurt your poor hands. OK?'

Rebecca pivoted away from the tent. Jacob marched off with her. She shot him a stern look. Jacob pushed his lips together and topped them with his fingers. He had indeed said more than enough.

Rebecca walked in silence, shoulders drooping.

'Mum,' Jacob tried to be pleading but kindly, 'Mum. What's got into you?'

'Nothing. I'm just tired. That's all.' Rebecca didn't look Jacob in the eye and didn't smile. Jacob knew something was wrong. She never walked with him to the big market without talking.

'You're quiet, Mum. Since when did my mother hold her tongue with me?'

'I'm just adjusting, that's all. Life moves on. We have to move on.' She sighed. Her words said she did not want sympathy but her manner called out for comfort.

'Mum, if you're thinking of adjusting to those Hittite harridans of Esau, please don't!' Jacob made his words earnest but cheerful.

'Maybe we brought it on ourselves? Now we are in an alliance with the Philistines, Esau has made an alliance with the Hittites. Perhaps it's all for some greater good.' Rebecca spat out her last word.

'Mum! A formal political alliance and a marriage are two different things! You can't say Esau negotiated on behalf of the whole community. He just went hunting for women, especially those who have big boobs, big bums and tiny brains.'

Rebecca did now smile and look at Jacob. She didn't tell him off for speaking ill of his newish sisters-in-law. 'But maybe he was thinking that this would help us be accepted round here. It's what they do. Bind the leaders, have children together, share traditions.' Rebecca was imitating Jeshach and his type.

'And you've seen their so-called traditions! Lying back and ordering their mother-in-law to massage their feet! "Oh! Don't you do that?" they say snootily. "Our families cherish their young women." Calling a male servant to help them with their body scarves, asking them to smooth the creases out of the curved parts of their front and then slapping them for their impertinence and giggling as the poor lad flees as quickly as he can. If that's tradition they can keep it!'

Rebecca looked warmly at Jacob. He knew she knew he understood.

'And do you really think Esau thought it all through? Maybe he thought that now we are settled, that gave him licence to have any sort of wife he fancies.'

'It's not just that they have their own ways,' Rebecca confided, drawing a little closer to Jacob. 'It's also that there are two of them! Why can't he be satisfied with one, right at the beginning? Doesn't he know his father's great decision? Can't he see the rivalry? It's everywhere, not just with Ishmael...' Rebecca wrung her hands and sighed.

Jacob was taken aback. 'But two wives from our people would have been all right? It's not exactly rare!'

'Your father!' flared Rebecca, 'Your father, bless him, could see the bitterness, the nastiness, the quarrels, all because his father had two wives, or at least two mothers of his children! Your father's children were never going to have to go through that! Now his grandchildren will have to.'

'You feel strongly about this,' demurred Jacob. 'It's really that important?'

'Important!' Rebecca's flare was now a blaze. 'Children living in harmony isn't important? Men being faithful to one woman isn't important? Men learning to become true partners, men learning to control their lust and their wandering eyes, men learning to hold to their decisions – you think that's not important?'

Jacob blinked and decided silence was the wisest response.

'Oh Jakey! I thought you could see all these things.'

His mother's voice was softer, more wistful. 'Aren't they obvious? Don't you see the damage done by competing wives, children, tribes? Definitely in our neighbours, but also in our people. Oh God, open his eyes!' Rebecca looked up. 'You are the Faithful One. Teach my son what it means to be faithful like you!'

Jacob allowed a reverential pause. 'He probably just fancied two women in his bed,' jested Jacob, diverting the conversation.

Rebecca looked stern.

'Come on!' Jacob continued, 'Surely you've heard them? They don't always wait for the night. Esau comes back after 4 days hunting and it's all giggles and grunts and gasps by the three of them!'

Rebecca shook her head, smiling. She spoke quietly, conspiring. 'You can't say they are strong on discretion. Or on cooking. Or on cleaning anything. They'd rather put on some sickly oil than have a proper wash. And the incense they burn to their little statues! Now there are boobs and bums and little else for you!'

Jacob laughed. 'It's OK, Mum. They can't hear. They can't cope with our dialect!' Rebecca laughed along. Both Judith and Basemath had made a big deal of looking blank whenever they were asked to fetch some water or take a turn at looking after some goats. They would then give a cheesy smile and go back to their house. The giggles that soon followed were so annoying.

'Seriously, though,' said Jacob, 'sex and fertility are their aim in life, nothing more. Esau has to 'sow his seed' in them in order to get any kind of fruit from his labours. If the hunting goes well, it's thanks to them and he has to perform for them again. If it goes badly, it's because he hasn't pleased them enough and he has to try harder. Do they really need him to pay for more massage oils? They have him hooked. No wonder he sometimes looks exhausted!'

Jacob was enjoying letting out his vindictive thoughts, even if he was exaggerating. 'As far as I'm concerned it's not "all for the good" at all. We need to keep them and their ways at arm's length. If only we could quarantine them! You certainly don't have to pander to them. Even Dad seems less enamoured of Esau now.'

'He says it can all work out for the best.' Rebecca sighed. 'He's so polite to them when sometimes I just want to slap them. It's hard to know what he sees and what he doesn't see.'

'But he's not been as cheerful. You probably haven't noticed because it's all brought you down so much. I don't think he's enjoying his daughters-in-law any more than you are.'

'The Hittites are important to him. "Any friend of Ephron is a friend of mine." You've heard him say that.'

Jacob nodded. He had heard often about how good Ephron the Hittite had been to sell part of his land, mostly only a cave, to Grandad Abraham. This was now the family burial place. Apparently, it was a big deal that a Hittite sold some of his ancestral land, especially to a new-coming nomad from way away in the East.

'Do you really think that Beeri and Elon are the proteges of Ephron as they make out?' Both Judith's and Basemath's fathers had stressed how close they were to the much-esteemed Ephron, although they seemed to know surprisingly little about him. They were vague about where the cave was.

Rebecca frowned a little as she thought.

'Something my mother hasn't thought of!' said Jacob in triumph. 'I think Dad has seen through them. He's having serious second thoughts. Talk to him. I'm sure your view of the Hittite hormone horses is much the same as his.'

'Thanks, Jacob,' said Rebecca, looking more relaxed.

'Jeshach, what does my father think of Esau's wives?' Jacob was sitting with his father's Advisor sampling the mint tea for Jeshach's family and guests.

Jeshach leaned back and smiled. 'One could imagine the response of your perceptive mother, sir. She may take it that you were making matrimonial musings yourself, sir?'

Jacob blushed despite himself. 'My question is about what my father is thinking. I am sure he expresses himself more freely to you.'

'Yes indeed, sir.' Jeshach removed the smile from his face. 'Though your father does not always confide in detail to me, sir.'

'What have you picked up?' insisted Jacob. 'What impression does he give?'

'To be frank, sir, I have rarely seen your father so troubled as now.' Jeshach sighed. 'How much this is caused by the extended family circumstances, and how much due to other factors, is hard to determine. One could observe, with some bewilderment, that, now that the immediate anxieties of life are considerably less, a more general anxiety has affected our leader. I trust that his natural ebullience will be more evident before long, sir.'

'You think he is anxious about the prancing pair?'

'I am sure you have observed, sir, that, for some time, your father's eyesight has not been as acute as before.' Jeshach looked concerned. 'This, and the awareness of his general mortality, seem to be having a depressing effect on his mood.'

'Being reminded of Grandad's grave, courtesy of the Hittites, can't help!' shot out Jacob.

'And, if I may say so, sir, being aware of the barely concealed animosity borne by one of his sons to the partners of the other, does not have an uplifting effect either, sir.' Jeshach eyeballed Jacob, eyebrows raised briefly.

'Come on Jeshach!' countered Jacob. 'He hasn't exactly welcomed them with open arms himself.'

'It is all a matter of degree and decency, sir. Hospitality is always important. A reputation for welcoming the stranger pays dividends in the long term, especially when one could say that we are currently in deficit in our hospitality account, having received from the Philistines more than we contributed.'

Jacob was about to cut in again but Jeshach raised his hand.

'Relations with the local peoples are complex, sir. The last situation in which we desire to find ourselves is at war with the Hittites. So, holding back from animosity towards our Hittite residents, guests with a prestigious invitation, is a wise restraint, despite some continuing concern, sir, as to the wisdom of the particular relationship through which we are bound to them and they to us, sir.'

'Go on,' encouraged Jacob. 'What concern?'

'Now that you understand the context and the need to be careful, indeed caring, in these matters, sir,' Jeshach paused for effect, 'one can also observe that an alliance such as that contracted by your brother has implications for the future of our family, for our particular attitudes and approaches to life, for our loyalty to the One, indeed. Living in harmony with the local peoples is a situation to be earnestly desired. This harmony can helpfully be strengthened by a political alliance, such as that obtaining between the Philistines and ourselves, which recognises and affirms our distinct cultures, sir. An alliance which can, and probably will, blur the distinctions through a more intimate mingling of family ways, family devotions, family practices, is less to be desired indeed, sir.'

'Have you talked about this with Esau?' challenged Jacob 'I can't imagine he has thought it through.'

'Yes indeed, sir. Your father, I am sure, would have wished to have had this kind of conversation before the bringing and binding of the Hittite ladies in question. No doubt he is considering how to address the situation now that the alliance has taken place. This may well be contributing to his overall concern, sir.'

'And two wives make double trouble?' Jacob looked gloomy.

Jeshach nodded, pursing his lips. 'I am glad, sir, that you can see the increased influence of the combined ladies. One, with a tenuous or strained connection with her people may be embraced and assimilated happily without altering the family substantially. Two, with a strong and proud connection with their people, bolstered by their very companionship and desire to show loyalty to their family, constitutes a challenge far more significant and serious, indeed sir.'

'So it is even more of a problem than I thought.' Jacob looked sad.

'There is another concern, sir, about the bigamous, or shall we say bi-amorous, alliance which has been contracted and which we all have to accommodate, it seems. You know that your father is well known for his singular attachment to your mother?'

Jacob did not hesitate. 'Yes, of course.'

'Your father is convinced, partly through his early experience, that a family with competing wives is not a stable family, nor a successful, nor a happy one. And it is the nature of a multiple marriage to become a seed bed of rivalry, jealousy and even hatred. The promise of The One is, he believes, best embraced by a man who is happy, shall we say, with the one life-lady, however paltry such an achievement may appear in the eyes of other men.'

Jacob nodded. 'I see… But…' he continued with hesitation. 'What about Grandad Abraham marrying again? You know, Keturah and her sons?'

'Ah.' Now Jeshach responded with a slow nod. 'One can only say that actions do not always follow from words, even the wisest and most considered words. One could even say that your father's position on this matter, his championing of one wife rather than many, derives as much from his experience of that later marriage of his father as from the earlier misalliance which affected him more directly.'

'You make him sound more stern than he seems.' Jacob could still not take in such an apparently vehement stance from such an easy-going man.

'Again, sir, it is a mistake to expect a firm conviction to be expressed in a dictatorial manner. One may find, rather, that those who are convinced of a conclusion, through bitter experience and careful reflection, are so settled in their mind and heart that the position seems unchallengeable and not in need of urgent and insistent defence.'

Jacob rolled his eyes and took a deep breath.

'May I ask you also to consider your father's behaviour in this matter? Do you think that, in the times of friendship and prosperity with our Philistine hosts, there was never an opportunity for, indeed an attraction from, a younger and obviously desirable lady? Or do you think that, in the earlier years of waiting, praying, beseeching for a child from his stubbornly barren wife, the straightforward option of fatherhood through alliance with a comely and considerate woman was never presented to your father?

Jacob nodded half up and down, half side to side. 'Yes, I can see that.' He did not sound convinced.

'Please continue, sir,' said Jeshach with emphasis, 'to consider this choice which your father has made and would be delighted to see adopted by one of his sons.'

'OK. OK.' Jacob sighed. 'So Esau's made a bad choice in many ways, and we have to grin and bear it.'

'Your father will be pleased and relieved to know that you embrace his viewpoint on this matter, sir,' Jeshach's words were slow. After a pause, he continued, 'I shall convey to him your understanding of his concern about this matter and of the need not to exacerbate the problem with any intemperate remarks, sir?'

'Go ahead Jeshach,' breezed Jacob. 'You hardly need my permission.'

CHAPTER SIX

The Blessing and the Deception

(Genesis 27:1 – 28:5)

'Jacob, listen!' Rebecca rushed into the store room. 'Put down the scales. Forget what you were doing. Just listen!'

'OK, OK! If the sky really is falling, if the locusts are coming, I'm listening!' Jacob smiled at his overwrought mother with her scrawny gesticulating arms, her brown working robe with the short sleeves, her high-cheeked face, her desperate look.

'Jacob, it's serious! When have you known me to play act? Your father is preparing to give the blessing to Esau! I've just heard him. "Go and hunt for me. A good wild deer. Get it prepared as I like it, good and tasty. The deer will be a bond between us, and I'll bless you. Not an ordinary blessing. THE blessing, the final one before I die."

'Die? He's still laughing as loud as he ever has!'

'Does that matter? This is THE blessing, and he wants to give it to Esau!' Rebecca was exasperated, but tried hard to calm herself. 'It's his eyes, poor man. He knows he'll never regain his sight. It makes him think he's on that last slope down.' She looked at Jacob, wide-eyed, appealing.

'How did Esau trick him into that? Selfish schemer!' Taking advantage of a weakened man.' Jacob sighed. 'But it seems too late to do anything about it.'

Rebecca laughed, somewhat to Jacob's surprise. Then came the tirade. 'Too late! Your brother is going to get the blessing. What will you get? Do you want him to be the one? Do you want us to become a caravan of hunters? Do you want the blessing to enrich those women? Jacob, wake up!'

Jacob blinked and looked at his mother as he would look at a whirling dust storm, not something he could influence.

'Listen, my son Here's what you have to do. Just follow what I tell you to do. We can turn this round.'

Jacob carried on looking. Interjecting felt too dangerous.

'Go to the animals. Go and choose, for me, two good kids. You slaughter them. I'll cook them, just as your father likes, good and tasty. You then take them to your father. He'll eat your animals and he'll bless you. Then, whenever he dies, you'll be the blessed one.'

Jacob paused, testing how safe it was to speak. 'Blessed? Cursed more like. He'll know I'm not Esau. He just has to touch my smooth skin, nothing like Esau's hairy arms. He'll know I'm trying to trick him. He'll be furious. No blessing, a curse instead.'

'Any curse will be mine, let it fall on me.' said Rebecca

earnestly. 'You just go. Do what I tell you. Get the goats for me.' She appealed to Jacob, her eyes wide. Jacob raised his eyebrows and returned his mother's gaze. Maybe he could mess up, take over, his swaggering brother's plan?

Jacob went. Part of him felt that he was doing an errand for his mother as he had done many times before. She wanted a couple of young goats; she would have them. Part of him knew that this wasn't for her at all. She needed him to select and slaughter, she needed them to be his goats, as much as Esau's deer were his deer. Jacob tried to think they were for her. He was also aware he was more eager to get his hands on the animals, to get in in front of the brother who wanted to push him out.

It wasn't hard to choose two. One speckled, one with large colour patches, both with bright, healthy eyes between their floppy ears. Jacob lured them away with some figs, soon had some thick string round their necks. He braced himself, took hold of the butchering knife, checked it was sharp, gave one goat another mouthful of figs and, standing behind its shoulder, holding up its gobbling head, slashed its throat. The second one became a little jumpy but accepted the figs and the fate. Jacob had never become used to this part of their life. It didn't come naturally as it seemed to come to bloody Esau.

Jacob took the carcases to his mother, and went to wash while she took off the skins and cooked the meat, good and tasty for Isaac. As he washed, Jacob thought about the strange combination which everyone took for granted – blood and blessing. Was it an exchange in the grand scheme of things, one life taken in order for another life to be enhanced? Was it simply a payment to The One for the aforesaid blessing? What was the bond between the person who killed the animal and the person who ate the meat? What kind of animal bridge was this over which blessing could be conveyed? Jacob didn't have the instinctive sense of God and what God wants, that his mother, and his father, had in their different ways. He had too many questions.

Jacob did know one thing. He needed the blessing. Esau could happily manage on his own. Esau relished taking the initiative, men followed him naturally, with his strong arms and piercing eyes and bluff humour. Why did people not see through the stupid swagger? Men were impatient with Jacob. They respected him as Isaac's son, but his words were just a little too hesitant, his manner a little too pleading, his physique a little too weedy. He was greeted warmly, people talked of him as a 'nice lad.' But he had to work hard to convince them to do things they would have done for Esau at the drop of a hint.

If Jacob needed to move ahead in life, he needed someone or something to pull him along. He could feel himself being pulled along by his mother at this moment. He trusted her enough to let it happen. If she pulled him into the place where he had the extra support, the blessing, that he needed, who was he to refuse? The Philistine king's words had taken root in his head. 'We have seen an invisible hand guiding you, protecting you, blessing you.' Jacob had to have this hand blessing him. He just didn't have it in him to make a go of life on his own. Did it matter how the blessing came? His mother was confident that his father could be deceived. She knew him a lot better than Jacob did. And he did want to stop Esau in his tracks. What about the One? Would he just go along with it? His mother must have thought about that too; she knew more about their God than most people. He could almost hear her saying 'You can think too much, Jakey. Just listen to me!'

'Keep still!' Jacob's mother snapped at him. 'Or you'll feel the needle.'

'But' Jacob turned round suddenly. 'Where did you get Esau's best clothes from?' He felt that he had woken up from sleep-walking. He'd put his arms in the embroidered shirt like a five-year-old overawed by going to his first wedding. It felt strange, smelt oddly familiar. Suddenly he realised what was happening was not as straightforward as he had been told.

Rebecca dropped her hands to her sides and sighed in exasperation. 'They were here. Esau left them here for ironing. His wives may be good at some things but for them you have to be lying down, mostly.' She smiled, pleading for Jacob to join the fun at the expense of the awful foreign women.

Jacob pulled his head back and furrowed his brow. He paused to show that he was not sure about taking in this story. 'Since when have you done their work for them? You've been planning this for a long time...' Jacob wanted to register that he wasn't going along with the charade wholeheartedly. But he kept the shirt on. He wasn't not going along with it either.

'You prefer your own half-baked, or non-existent,

scheme? How else are you going to secure the blessing, my son?' Rebecca looked at him with kindness and challenge. Jacob looked back, saying nothing, nodding gently. His stomach, though, was churning and his bladder was strangely piercing. That part of him desperately wanted to run away for a break, as though running from a lion's roar. He steeled himself and clenched his fists. The costume was not going to take long.

Rebecca went behind Jacob, gathered up the extra inches of shirt and ran her needle through the cloth, humming an old tune.

'Now you were right, my boy. Skin counts. Your father will want to touch your hands. We can get round that. It's a good thing Esau's so hairy, very very hairy.' She made it sound like a jokey song.

Jacob put on a frown rather than a responding smile. But no more protest.

'Hold out your hand, now,' Rebecca spoke with happy confidence. Her Jakey was not going to rebel against her now. She put strips of kid's skin on his hands, and round his lower arms so that the wide sleeves of Esau's shirt overlapped them. 'Bend forward,' she commanded matter-of-factly. Jacob tried to think this was like having his hair cut, tried not to think of his father patting the back of his neck as he liked to pat Esau's neck. He bent forward and felt the animal skin being tucked deftly over his shoulders so it covered the patting place. He had bowed obediently and, he had to admit later, knowingly.

'Stand up straight!' Rebecca said, not for the first time in his life. She nodded, satisfied. Without a word she held out to him the bowl with the stew and the plate with bread she had baked. Jacob took them. Rebecca smiled. Jacob looked at her expecting her to say something else, but she seemed content with her last words. She wasn't now telling Jacob what to do. He had gone too far for that. He walked on, trying to push out his chest and lengthen his stride, Esau-like.

'My father!' Jacob called out in his deepest possible voice, wondering at the same time how long he could keep up this acting. 'Here's your...' he stumbled, his voluminous shirt briefly snagged in the door frame, dropping bread and the stew lid onto the floor. All was quickly back where it should be. 'My father!' repeated Jacob, a little more breathlessly.

'Here I am,' said Isaac straining to look in the direction of the voice. 'Who are you, my son?'

'I am Esau, your first born,' said Jacob gruffly. The words came out simple and easy and lying. 'I've done what you told me.' Jacob coughed to lower his voice again. 'Please get up. Sit and eat my game, for your blessing to come to me.' It was a relief after the big lie, to slip back into words he meant for himself.

'Here already!' said Isaac with a chuckle of surprise. 'How did you find it so quickly?'

'Because The One, your God, sent it across my path.' Jacob was glad he had thought of this answer already.

'Please come near,' said Isaac to Jacob more seriously 'so I can touch you, my son, and know that you are my own son Esau, or not.'

Jacob took a short deep breath. There was no way out now. This was the end of everything. How could his father not tell the difference between kid's skin and Esau? He walked up to his father Isaac. Isaac pulled up his arm and patted his hand.

'The voice is the voice of Jacob,' Isaac said, puzzling. Jacob's heart sank. After all that effort! Jacob was stunned, silent, waiting to be slaughtered for his deception. 'But the hand is the hand of Esau.' Isaac spoke with manly confidence. Mum's hairy hands had worked. He really did feel like Esau. 'Thank God!' said Isaac. Jacob half relaxed. He couldn't be completely sure what was going on in his father's mind.

'Are you really Esau?' asked Isaac, squinting through his large clouded eyes. Had Jacob relaxed, maybe sighed, too much? He quickly gathered himself again. 'I am' affirmed Jacob, gruff once again and determined to say as little as possible now.

'Bring it on!' said Isaac with a hint of a grin. 'And I will eat my son's game, to bless you with a full heart.'

Jacob was relieved and tried not to show it this time. He brought the meat and his father ate, chewing too slowly for Jacob's comfort, but with clear satisfaction. 'What if he asks me more about the hunting?' thought Jacob. 'If only I had worked out more of a story!' He tried to think of the hunting words he had heard, animals tacking left or right, taking them down, blooded. He looked around nervously, grateful that he did not need to hide his facial expressions, in front of his weak-eyed father.

Jacob brought wine and his father drank. 'He's not

saying anything! Why not? Doesn't he usually chat with Esau?' Jacob wondered again about talking about the weather, or asking how the food was. Would this be less nerve-wracking than the silence? 'Don't take the risk!' he told himself. His attempts to disguise his voice had not worked. He kept quiet, his fingers fidgety, his neck itchy, under the goat skin.

His father spoke. 'Come near' he said gently, 'and kiss me, my son.' He emphasised 'my son' even more. Did he always talk with Esau this way, not using his name?

Jacob came near and kissed him on his cheek. He couldn't remember when he had last been so close to his father. It made him feel like a little boy again, although now his father was not the giant at the edge of his life. Isaac inhaled deeply. 'Thank God!' said Isaac with contentment. 'Ah! The smell of my son is like a field blessed by The One.' Jacob felt his father's hand heavy on the top of his head. 'To you may God give of the dew from heaven, and the fatness of the land, and plenty of grain and oil.' Another pause. Jacob's head felt warm. It seemed that the blessing was coming to him! 'Keep calm, stand tall, you're still Esau as far as he knows,' he told himself. His father's voice continued, confident, loud. 'May peoples serve you and nations bow down to you. Be lord of your brothers, be obeyed by the sons of your mother. Cursed be those who curse you and blessed be those who bless you, my son, my dear son!'

Jacob felt his hair being ruffled, then his head released. He felt suddenly light, his hair strangely smooth. His father's hand then pushed him forward a little. He father settled back contentedly, with a little chuckle.

Jacob managed to mutter in a deep voice 'Thank you, Father, I'll leave you to rest now.' He hurried out before his father could try to engage him in any conversation.

'So how did it go? So what did he say? So…?' Rebecca had her hands in the air in front of her as she looked at Jacob with her eyes and mouth open wide.

'Ph.., Phhh…,' exhaled Jacob. 'I'm exhausted!' He slumped on a stool. 'Wine! Do you have any wine?'

'Men!' muttered Rebecca under her breath, as she bustled away and returned with a cup of wine. She watched intently as Jacob drank. 'So now you can talk?'

'The voice is the voice of Jacob,' Jacob recounted gloomily, 'but the hand, and the smell, is of Esau. Oh my goodness, it was touch and go.' He paused and then brightened. 'Literally! He touched me and it was on. Yes, mother, in the end, he blessed me. Thank you.'

'He blessed you!' Up came her hands again, with her smiling lips. 'Jacob, my boy.' Great tenderness from her heart calming her down. 'You are the blessed one. Just as it should be.' She smiled at him and then stood by him, left arm around his shoulder, right hand on his head, ruffling his hair gently. 'Blessed indeed! It's not been easy, I know, I know. You'll be fine now.'

'Well, it's thanks to you, Mum.' Jacob looked up at Rebecca and smiled. 'I really thought he'd seen through the disguise. Without the goat skin, I'd have been found out for sure.'

'What does it matter now? You have the blessing! Enjoy it!' She lifted her hands from him and stood a little in front of him, her hands wiping her apron. 'So what did he say?'

'He said I'd have plenty of grain and wine, and people, brothers,' Jacob paused and looked pointedly at his mother, 'brothers would obey me.' He looked pensive. 'Brothers, my mother's sons. How many do you have?'

'Brothers indeed! One is enough for you!' Rebecca chuckled. 'Grain and wine for you, my boy, just as it should be, eh?'

Jacob looked at her a little puzzled. 'It's just the blessing you would expect, isn't it? Nothing special.'

Rebecca looked at her son, pausing, her lips curled up with a hint of cheekiness. 'Your blessing, my boy.'

'Even if it was meant for Esau!' Jacob waggled his head in pride at giving his sneering brother his comeuppance.

'Would Esau have been happy with grain and wine – and the work of producing them?' Rebecca looked more serious.

Jacob held his head still, eyes wider open.

'Does your father really not know the difference between his son's hair and a goat's?' Rebecca raised her eyebrows. 'Are his fingers now feeling dimly? Or does he not want to know? Was he secretly happy to bless his younger son with stores of grain and wine?' Rebecca tilted her head to her left, eyebrows still up.

Jacob blinked. Had his father been deceived or not? This was a question too far, beyond his capacity now. Too much had happened today.

Rebecca breathed deeply. 'Now!' she became brusque

again. 'Off with that ridiculous shirt! Stop pretending to be a goat. Did I ever tell you when your father had to be a goat? Never mind, that's another story. Come on! That sounds like Esau's back already.'

Esau was back from hunting. He also cooked tasty food, with the help of a couple of servants, and brought it to his father. 'Get up, my father,' said Esau. 'Now eat your son's game, that your blessing may come to me!'

'Who are you?' said Isaac hesitantly.

Esau did not hide that he thought this a ridiculous question. 'I am your son. Your first-born. Esau.'

Isaac's hands started trembling. His chest laboured to breathe. His head went into great spasms. He opened his mouth a couple of times and then managed to say: 'Who?' Once the question was out, he could breathe a little better. 'Who hunted game and brought it to me and I ate it all, before you came, and I blessed him?' He breathed deeply and shook his head. 'Yes. Blessed. He is…' his voice tailed off.

Esau cried out loud and bitter and strong. 'What? Him? How?' He grabbed his father's arm and demanded, 'Bless me also my father!'

'Your brother came sneakily,' said Isaac, still trembling a little, 'and has taken away your blessing. It's gone.'

'Jacob! Even his name means he takes other people's places. This is the second time he's taken my place! He took my birth-right from me and now he's taken my blessing!' Esau looked at his father, pleading, suddenly no longer the big man. 'Don't you have a blessing kept back for me?'

Isaac spoke to Esau grimly, tenderly. 'I have made him your master and all his brothers are to be his servants. I have given him grain and wine to sustain him. And now...?' Isaac sighed. 'What shall I do?'

'Blessing,' Isaac continued pleading. 'Have you only one, my father? Bless me, also me, my father!' Isaac cried out, groans and tears.

Isaac looked at him with answering tears. His cloudy eyes then turned away, upwards, straining to see something else. 'So, you shall see. Away from the fatness of the land shall you find home, away from the dew of heaven above. By your sword shall you live, and your brother shall you serve.' Isaac paused. He moved his head side to side a little as though he had caught a glimpse of something he wanted to see more clearly. 'There will come a time of dominion for you! You shall break his yoke from your neck.' Isaac slumped.

'That can't come too soon!' shouted Esau as he stormed out.

Rebecca had told Esau's servants that it would be to their advantage to keep her informed about Esau.

'Bastard! Snivelling, conniving, toad! Jacob!' Esau spat out the hated name, striding up and down in his house. 'He gets the blessing! Ridiculous! He's not strong enough to lead one goat, let alone this whole family group. He'll be a disaster!' Esau was shouting.

'Esee, dear,' said Judith soothingly. 'What's matter?'

Esau flinched a little at his least favourite nickname. 'It's my brother that's the matter! He's taken my place. He's taken my blessing. Now I'll be second best – or worse!'

'No, no you worry. Come here!' Basemath held out her arms for Esau, while looking at Judith.

'Look, it's serious!' Esau looked at both wives, from a little distance. 'He'll be in charge. No-one will respect him. He won't be able to stand up to anyone. '

'This impossible,' said Judith. 'You big man, you first son. You leader. Everyone know.'

'It's not impossible! Don't you hear? It's happened?' Esau slumped onto a large cushion.

'Everyone know you first son and first son always leader.' Judith was not giving up.

Esau groaned. 'Not in this family. We don't always do what everyone else does. Can't see why we have to make up our own rules. Do you think Dad was the first born? You've heard of Ishmael? He was born first and he's been kicked out of the family.'

'But you, Esee, you strong one.' Basemath cajoled. 'People want strong man, people follow strong man.'

'Ha! Don't you know Ishmael could knock Dad down in any contest he chose? It's not the way things work here. Selection of the strongest? Selection of the weakest, more like.' Esau shook his head in sad frustration. 'I should have seen this coming. Dealt with him properly before now. We can't live with this!'

'You strong man. You "deal with him." He afraid you.' Judith spoke calmly and forcefully, her voice husky. 'My husband, my warrior. You can do anything. You true man!'

She knelt down in front of him, her hands on the ground, her breasts heaving a little.

Basemath also knelt down next to Esau and rubbed his arm, kneading his muscle. 'Big strong man. Everyone like strong man. Everyone follow strong man.'

'Not now,' said Esau relaxing a little. 'Not while Dad is still around. He can think he's won, sneaky Jakey. Wait for the opportunity. Then strike! Break his yoke indeed. I'll kill him!'

Rebecca heard that Esau was planning a kill. She called Jacob.

'Look! Esau's mad. He's soothing himself with talk of killing you. You must do what I tell you. Don't stay here. Get away to Laban.' Jacob looked puzzled. 'My brother! In Haran! Stay a while with him.' Jacob looked at her as though she were crazy. 'A few days! Until your brother's rage passes. Until he finds another target, not you. He forgets! Including what you have done to him.' Rebecca raised her hands in front of her and smiled into Jacob's eyes.

Jacob looked at her, dazed. So it was all his doing now. He'd known that it would bring a curse on him. He was the blessed one and he was the one who had to run for his life! Was it worth it?

'And then, I'll send for you to come.' Rebecca made a beckoning motion with both hands.

'God knows when that's going to be,' said Jacob glumly. He held back from asking his mother about her promise to let the curse fall on her. Was the One angry too? Couldn't she tell people that it was all her doing? But could the blessing then be retracted? It was all too complicated. 'Isn't there...? Can't we...?' Jacob couldn't finish his sentences. He shook his head.

'Jacob!' Rebecca barked, but with tears in her eyes and voice. 'Why should I lose both of you in one day? You're going. All right?'

'Ah..., Becky dear!' said Isaac.

Rebecca bent over and kissed Isaac, lingering a little. 'We need to talk, dear.'

'Becky, my jewel. You always want to talk!' said Isaac, chuckling.

'It's good to see you laughing again,' said Rebecca. She had left it just long enough for his good humour to bubble up again. She didn't understand how it happened, almost by itself, but she had learnt to rely on it. Tasty food and only good news about the wells and the crops helped.

'So let me hear your sparkling voice,' encouraged Isaac.

'Jacob, our son,' said Rebecca sighing a little, testing his reaction to the name of the cheat who, said Esau, had distressed his father so deeply.

Isaac shook his head. 'Jacob indeed! Who would have thought he had it in him, eh, Becky? You've spent more time with him. Where did he get his scheming from?'

'Jakey?' Rebecca tried to keep her voice steady and cheerful. Was Isaac's question an accusation? 'He has a head on his shoulders, dear.' She hoped her emphasis on he, his, was not overdone. 'He can work things out. Deep things, far ahead things. And he knows the right time. A time to plant, a time to wait, a time to make his move.' Had she managed to convey safely that it was all Jacob's doing?

Isaac shook his head, wondering. 'Jacob! I never really thought of him as the front runner, not with those spindly legs.' He chuckled again, seeing memories clearer now than the people in front of his eyes. 'Now he has the blessing he wanted. Perhaps he's stronger than I thought.'

Rebecca relaxed, keen to change the subject a little. 'I wanted to ask you about that?' Rebecca felt bolder than she had expected. 'Did you intend to bless Esau with grain and wine, not gazelle and boar?'

Isaac frowned, puzzled. 'You know me! 'The One will provide!' I can still hear my father saying it. Even when it all looks like a dead end, we know who has the last laugh!' His chuckle bubbled up into a jolly laugh. 'I know better than to intend.'

'So there was your son in front of you, as you had asked,' encouraged Rebecca. 'and you had no idea what to say? I wish I had your confidence.'

'It felt that it was all going to be fine. A nice meal, good company, though a little quiet, some blessing. What's to worry? When it came to it, I was thrown, I must admit. I thought I was just being too suspicious. It was almost like being trapped. I couldn't get out of it, even if I did think something was wrong. He was so desperate, like he was hauling it out of me. The fields and the vineyards just came to me, someone holding open a sack as grain was poured in, poured in, a couple of people tipping a large jar as wine poured out… Then the people kneeling, prostrate, all kinds of people, our folk, foreigners, dressed like servants, dressed like masters, all in this amazing light, so bright! Then it faded. And he had what he wanted!' Isaac shook his head. 'He has some determination; I can say that for him.'

'Jacob pretending to be Esau. Who would have thought?' said Rebecca supressing a smile. 'Though do you think it might work for both of them? Could Esau be blessed also because you meant the blessing for him? They are both our sons.'

'You're deep, my jewel! Where do you find these questions?' Out came Isaac's chuckle again. 'I was so shocked by what Jacob had done and what came to Esau wasn't anything like as good. What will the One do with this all? Are we to know?'

'Well,' said Rebecca, pleased that she seemed to be in the clear. Her job wasn't going to be as difficult as she had expected. 'If Jacob's going to have all this blessing, he going to have to have a wife at his side.' She snuggled closer to him and clasped his hand warmly. 'A good woman. A jewel for Jacob! Now where will we find such a woman for him?'

Before Isaac could answer, Rebecca ended her pause. 'No! Don't say it! Did God provide those Hittite harpies? They're no blessing. My life! It's a headache having them in the family. Talk about weary! Just coping with their gossip, let alone finding all the treats they say they need. If Jacob marries a Hittite like them, a woman from this place… Why me? Why live?' Rebecca pleaded, sobbing a little, while she kept snuggled close.

'Becky love. That's not going to happen. My wife,'

142

he hugged her strongly, 'is the best! She's beautiful and gracious and smart. My son needs a wife like her, from the same background.'

Rebecca nodded. She couldn't have put it better herself. Sometimes, now, after all these years of marriage, she didn't even have to hint at what she wanted.

'Call him,' said Isaac, for once looking stern.

Jacob was called. Esau, along with everyone else, knew the summons. Everyone also knew, or had heard a rumour about, Jacob stealing the blessing. There were plenty of eyes, some half hidden, on Jacob as he made his way to his father, shoulders down, ready for the full dressing-down.

'Jacob!' said Isaac, with a little 'listen to me or else' anger in his voice.

'Yes sir.' Jacob was not intending to say any more than he had to.

'Thank God for you!' Isaac said more warmly, and paused.

Jacob wondered what this meant. It sounded better, much more accepting, than he had expected. Yet it sounded a little like a farewell. Was Jacob no longer welcome, or even tolerated, and this was his father's, somewhat kindly, way of pushing him away?

'Listen to me,' said Isaac. He looked serious, although the effect was muffled by him looking in Jacob's general direction rather than into his eyes. 'You are not to take a Canaanite wife! Do not marry a local woman. Go out! Go to Paddan-Aram. Go and see Bathuel, your mother's father, and find a wife for yourself there. One of the daughters of Laban, your mother's brother.'

Jacob nodded, then remembered his father couldn't see. 'Yes, sir. Thank you, sir.'

Isaac grinned. He couldn't keep up the seriousness for long. His anger really had passed. He was smiling again. Jacob could see the evidence but couldn't quite believe it.

'Come here!' Isaac spoke with more affection than Jacob could remember. Jacob came and sat on the stool next to his father, as indicated. Isaac put his arm round his son's shoulder and looked up with his misty eyes. 'May God the bountiful bless you,' he said with joy.

'No pretending this time,' thought Jacob. 'I wonder what meagre blessing will be mine now.'

'May God make you fruitful, grant you many children. May you become a great number of peoples. May he give you the blessing of Abraham! To you and to your children with you. May you take full possession of the land where you have lived, here and around, the land which God gave to Abraham.'

Jacob blinked. The words were hugely better than he had expected. At first, they sounded like a wedding blessing, as though his father could see the couple in front of him. Then the great family blessing, the dream of a secure homeland, this land, for himself and his children. Esau was not in the picture. Jacob knew that his father was famous for accepting what had happened, seeing the hand of The One as capable of bringing good out of everything. Here he was treating Jacob almost as the one who was always meant to be blessed.

'Off you go now!' said Isaac. 'And I mean now.'

CHAPTER SEVEN

The Flight and the Dream

(Genesis 28:6-22)

'Jakey, I almost wish I was coming with you. But I'm needed here with your father more than ever.' Rebecca rubbed her hands together. Jacob recognised this as her 'cooking something up' motion. 'We'll make sure you're all right, you'll have some good people with you. A man from our family is not a lone beggar, he's a man of substance, with servants.'

'OK. So you're going to send me with people to keep an eye on me,' said Jacob grumpily.

'We' Rebecca emphasised that this was not only her doing. 'We want people, especially Laban who notices these things, to see you for the important man that you are. Don't be so dramatic! You will have companions, advisors, people to make fires for you.'

'OK, OK! I'll have an easier journey and you'll know I won't do anything stupid. Who are the minders?'

Rebecca frowned. 'Your father says you need an

ambassador. Laban is a tricky negotiator. He doesn't like letting go of anything or anyone. So you'll have Jeshach.' Jacob rolled his eyes. 'Think of yourself as the King, with his Prime Minister, remember?'

'I hope there'll be someone less influential as well. A few days alone with Jeshach and my ears will stop working.'

'Jeshach wanted to take along an assistant, like an apprentice. "To have the opportunity to develop the experience of a worthy young man who could grow into a fine asset to our decision-making processes would be most welcome, if that concurs with your aims in this business,"' Jacob smiled at the accurate impression of Mr Pompous. 'Do you know Caleb? Bright, intelligent, but a bit brusque as yet. This journey should help him see the sense of diplomacy.'

Jacob did know Caleb, Amos' son. His large eyes set in a thin face marked him out. Even though still a young man, the hair above his forehead was sparse. He made up for it by keeping bushy growths of dark brown hair above and just over his ears.

'Sounds fun! Mr Pompous and Mr Brusque. Both telling me what to do.'

'And I think you need someone to look after you, as I would do. Miriam is keen to go. I'm not sure she will be strong enough, so I'm sending an assistant with her too. Do you know Hannah?'

Jacob raised his eyebrows. 'I should be well fed at least.' Hannah had a reputation of having weak eyes, no good for fine work, for embroidery. She made up for it with her instinctive cooking, grabbing ingredients with her hands, letting a little run out apparently at random, but more likely with a great feel for what was too much. Her eyes did seem a little cloudy, looking intently under the shiny brown hair which she liked cut at her shoulders. The whole effect made her stand out as different, Maybe it would be good for her to have time away from her contemporaries who were too prone to talking about her behind her back.

Jacob gave a short, resigned, laugh. 'Well, it seems I don't have a choice. When do we leave?'

'Stones! What's the use of stones?' Jacob furiously kicked up dust in the twilight. He wanted to kick at least one of the stupid hard irregular sharp nasty pointless nuisances far into the distance. But he didn't know how to kick stones, wearing sandals, without hurting his feet.

It was the second evening since they had left home. Jacob had not slept well and his legs were hurting.

'Why? Why did I let the woman put me up to it?' Jacob muttered, not sure if he wanted anyone else to hear. It had seemed such a good plan, certainly a good purpose. To relieve brother Esau of the chafing yoke of nurturing one small plot of land, when he longs only to roam the plains and hills in freedom. To make sure that the blessing passes to someone who truly appreciates it.

It had all gone as mother-planned. He had the blessing, of grain and wine and leadership. It was a blessing on the settled farming life, not a blessing fit for Esau the roaming hunter. Had his father realised the deception, and accepted it at the time? He certainly seemed to have accepted it once it was done.

Esau had not accepted it. He cracked his knuckles and spat when Jacob was anywhere near. Their mother entreated him to listen but he brushed her aside. It could have been explained to him that he could now enjoy his outdoors life without the great burden of deciding what to plant, what to sell, and when. He would share in the produce as much as he liked. He would be honoured as the family guardsman. But no, his Hittite wives made him feel the shame of having to give way to his younger brother and filled his imagination with ridiculous scenarios of coming off second best. His hunter manhood was affronted. Revenge was needed and Jacob was the prey.

'Why did I let the woman push me into it? What good is the blessing now?' Jacob had nothing: only stones. What if cheating to gain the blessing brought a curse instead? Mum had said that the curse would be on her, but she hadn't been the one telling lies. What if the One was angry? How did they think they could get away with such deception? Deceiving his father was one thing, deceiving the Almighty a completely different level. How on earth could he be blessed in that land where he would always be in fear of Esau's vengeance? Could he get used to this wandering, outcast, life? Did he have it in him? Or would they all be better off without him?

Jacob kicked more dust. He sat down, stood up, walked quickly up a little rise, shouted, came back slowly with his shoulders down. He seemed to be about to sit down again and then headed off on another lonely, tetchy, meander. The twilight faded. The servants wrapped their cloaks more tightly round them. They chewed on dry bread and dates. When Jacob came near, they tried to interest him in food. He stared at them as though they had spoken a foreign language. Then he shouted 'What's the point?' and set off again. Clouds moved across the stars. The servants covered their heads for warmth and wondered if there would be any sleep tonight.

'Sir, Sir!' called Jeshach at last. 'Jacob, sir, please... Please can I make a suggestion?'

Jacob stopped and looked. He was annoyed and also worn out with the repetitive fretting in his head. 'Go on,' he said sullenly.

'Well, sir. It is night. Now I know we have no tent, but it is possible to sleep and gain strength for tomorrow's journey.'

'Possible maybe for idiots with thick skulls! Where the heck can anyone lay their head here?' Jacob threw his arm round at the blasted stony land.

'If I may be permitted an observation which I trust you will not find offensive?'

'That's all I need!' railed Jacob impatiently. Miriam gave him a look remarkably like that of his chiding mother. 'Oh, go on if you must.'

'Well, sir, we did look round a little earlier and we found a couple of flat stones, sir, not too thick. You will be most surprised, possibly, to know that such a stone, free of dust, makes a quite acceptable head rest, sir.'

'I've told you!' Jacob groaned impatiently. 'Maybe for thick-heads! And where did you get this pearl of wisdom from? It didn't have anything to do with my bone-headed brother, did it?'

'Well, actually,' began the servant apologetically.

'For God's sake, just listen to him!' shouted Caleb suddenly. 'Accept that you can learn something from others!'

Jacob glared back at Caleb and said nothing The sharp words seemed to have punctured Jacob's temper. 'So,' Jacob spoke more calmly though still with bad grace. 'You want me to lie down, for you to grab some sleep.'

'Lie down,' emphasised the second servant. 'And be still.' He looked Jacob calmly in the face. 'Sir.'

'You'll feel much better in the morning after a nice good sleep,' said Hannah as sweetly as she could, though looking at Caleb as much as at Jacob.

'There's no way I'm going to sleep,' said Jacob grumpily. 'Oh, give me one of your so wonderful stones.'

Jacob lay down. He kicked and shuffled. There was a loud cough from Jeshach. 'Oh, for God's sake!' muttered Jacob. But he did lie still. And the cloak they had put on him was heavy, heavier than expected. His legs went heavy too, his chest felt heavy, almost snug. His head looked up from the stone, breathing air that was surprisingly fragrant. He felt himself drifting off.

Jacob dreamed. In the stony dust next to him were two large posts of wood, with a cross-piece joining them. The posts rose above the cross-piece. Jacob followed the posts up and saw another cross piece and another. It looked like a ladder. Where was the top? What was it resting against?

Jacob looked further up. The ladder stretched to the

clouds and into the clouds. Lights like slow shooting stars were rising up the top of the ladder. He followed the ladder, the lights, until they disappeared into the heavens. Now lights were coming down the ladder too. At first pin pricks of golden light, they grew larger as they came down. Up and down, down and up, weaving between each other and around the ladder.

As the lights came closer, they appeared person shaped. Closer still, they were huge. Golden, bright, immense, yet airy. many with wings, impossible numbers of wings. Some wings were beating slowly, like an eagle soaring with minimal effort. Other wings waved, dancing or caressing the air more than propelling.

As the wings fanned the air, streams of golden specks spun slowly away, golden particles spreading out into space. Some weaved upwards like meandering sparks from a fire. Most fell down like bright rain enjoying the dance, in no hurry to land.

Open-eyed, Jacob turned his gaze up and down and around. As he peered at the great creatures, he saw blue and purple and crimson swirling in the air around them. He had never seen sky with such depth. Turning his attention to the golden specks, he saw circles of the same colours around each one, then spinning off, some slow, expanding, some fast and tight. The more he looked, the more he saw. Had he not noticed the colours at first or did they come, were they revealed, by his looking?

As the bright beings came close, thrilled vibrations pulsed through the air. Jacob couldn't help smiling. Closer still, he was scared. They were so big they would surely smother his head which lay far too close to the ladder. His head was stuck, fixed to the stone. The first one was about to envelop him. Its edge or cloak brushed his nose, then fell away to the right side of his head before rising again. The second brushed his forehead and fell to the left side. After the fifth had descended and risen again, and he could still breathe and see, Jacob relaxed.

In between the immense person-lights Jacob could see the ground next to his head. As the gold sparks touched earth, the blue, purple and crimson circles spread out like drops of water, turning a deep green as they flowed. The more golden creatures came, and went, the more sparks and circles kissed the earth, the more green covered everything. Wider and deeper, the green mottled with different shades. Blue-green and olive-green and fresh-grass-green and more greens than conceivable.

Each heavenly presence in turn lit up the ground around the bottom of the ladder. The plush green covering erupted into rainbows dancing, cavorting, luxuriating, wild and free and in perfect harmony. Then settled into the greens until the next light carrier reached earth.

Jacob focused on the rising angels, magnificent, majestic, mesmerising. He listened to the vibrations and found he could hear notes, high and deep, then tunes, bright and thrilling. The creatures brought music with them and showered music around them in and with the golden specks and the colour circles. The more he listened, the more music filled the sky.

Were there words? At first, he wasn't sure, then voice sounds began to form: 'Alleiy, Alleiy, Alle-i-i' 'Lu, lu, lui.' Happy and hearty and holy. 'Yah, Yah, Yi-Yah-A!' Deep and dense and delightful. The sounds joined and experimented, becoming a pattern 'Allelu... Yah. Allelui.., Ayah!' Jacob relaxed and smiled and relished the waves of harmony. More words appeared growing distinct in the air before finding partners: Suddenly they formed a sentence: 'God, you are good and your love is forever, Alleluia!'

Jacob was compelled to listen and watch. He wanted nothing more than to listen and watch. 'Wow, wow, wow!' Amazement filled his head and echoed in his whole body.

As Jacob gazed at the brilliant beings, a new voice appeared in the air, in harmony with the other voices but speaking more than singing It came not from the ladder, not from the sky, but from next to him, close by.

'I am, I am, the God of Abraham your father and the God of Isaac.' The voice was calm, almost gentle, fitting perfectly with the majestic angels. The heavenly beings paused and expanded. Already enormous, now they showed a new dimension of attention, both soldiers and listeners, alert to The Voice. With each phrase, each word, fresh rivers of golden sparks cascaded out from the angels, fresh circles of colour, thicker and deeper and more vibrant, spun into space.

'The land on which you are lying...' The green sea flowed effortlessly and effervescently and affectionately, bursting with more shades, a living kaleidoscope of hues. 'This land... I will give to you and to your offspring.' Jacob felt that he could lie here forever. The earth, even the stone, seemed to bend to fit his shape. He relaxed, supported, delighted to lie still. If he moved, he was sure to miss something. He didn't want his old straw mattress at all.

'Your offspring shall be like the dust of the earth; you shall spread far to the west and to the east and to the north and to the south.' Jacob now saw orange specks in clusters close to the ground near him, moving away from him. He realized they were coming from him. Like the heavenly sky sparks, these earthy dust balls flowed through and under the green covering in streams before multiplying, spreading out.

The voice was like an echo of the blessing of his father, or were his father's words an echo of this strong, steady, musical Voice? The Utterance continued: 'All the families of the earth shall be blessed in you and in your offspring.' The blessing was indeed with him! The blessing would flow from him and, unbelievably, from children to come. What of the curse of deception now?

As the word 'blessed' rang out like a bell, the dust balls glowed here and there with light. As far as Jacob could see from his low point of view, tiny lights flickered and shimmered. Even beyond the edge of the green sea, into the darkness beyond, pin points of orange glowed. As the earth lights spread out, angels flew from the ladder overshadowing. No gaps were left in the procession of light beings on the ladder which remained full.

After a pause, The Voice continued, stronger. 'Know!' The angels expanded yet more, more erect, more attentive. Jacob suddenly felt more awake. 'Know that...' What did he need to know? What had he forgotten? That The One cannot be deceived by a mere mortal? Jacob's stomach turned and he shivered.

'Know that I am with you…' At the word 'with' a warm gust wrapped itself around Jacob. The shivers melted. Jacob felt cosy, secure, as when his mother smiled to him or hugged him. The warmth attached itself to him. He knew that when he moved, the warmth would move with him, like the best-fitting cloak.

'And…!' Some angels put trumpet-horns to their heads. Two notes, deep and high, filled the sky, weaving through the sparks and circles. 'I will keep you, wherever you go!' The Voice could have been Jacob's mother's voice, or ten thousand mother's voices. Jacob realized he now had four angels around him, right and left, front and back. Those next to him lifted their wings over him, forming a canopy of gold feathers. The angel in front pulsed with golden light. Over him was a rainbow also stretching as a canopy a short way beyond, preparing the place for Jacob to walk. Jacob knew, more than saw, that the angel behind also carried a rainbow, covering Jacob's steps. He felt lighter, lifted, almost floating on a warm river.

'And…!' Four notes, deeper and higher than the first two, resounded. 'I will bring you back to this land.' Now orange dust balls were flowing towards Jacob as well as away, like the angels both falling and rising on the ladder. Flowing out and ebbing back as though borne on sea waves, the ball-specks rose and fell like birds enjoying their flight. Angels still covered their movement. Once again, Jacob felt the land under him, supporting, welcoming.

'I will not…' Six notes, more emphatic, awakened Jacob's attention again. The Voice seemed to be smiling. 'I will not leave you until I have done what I have promised you.' The motherly warmth wrapped around Jacob afresh. He wriggled, each muscle delighting in the embrace. The angel voices became a united torrent: 'Amen and Amen! It will be done! All will be well!' As the tremendous sound receded Jacob heard something like an echo of The Voice. Small and gentle and still, comforting words formed on the inside of his ears: 'Know that I am with you, wherever you go.'

When Jacob woke, the dream was still vivid. The ladder, the angels! The voice too. What a dream! What a promise! Was The One covering his anger for now? Or was Jacob convincing himself through his dreams that he would be all right?

What a place! A God place! Who would have thought it? It seemed so empty. He had missed it… Jacob felt foolish and small and overwhelmed. What if he missed, misread, similar places again? What if he stepped in the wrong place, disturbed any angels? How angry could The One be? He shivered, afraid.

Better give due respect to this place, Jacob thought. 'What an amazing place!' he burst out, breathless. 'God's place, God's house. Here. This place.' He looked round at the stones lit up on one side by the low rising sun. 'The gate of heaven!'

Jacob stood up. The servants were well awake, looking at him bemused. His mouth had given voice to his thought.

'Good morning, sir!' greeted Jeshach. 'We hear that, in some positive, even divine, way, you can see more good in this place. Seeing you with such reverence, makes this a good morning indeed, sir.'

With excitement and fear, Jacob told them his whole dream. 'What a place this is! We'll mark it! Gather stones, big ones at first. And what a stone this is!' He picked up the stone on which his head had slept. 'This, this dream-stone, will be on top!'

Jacob darted around inspecting stones. 'Come and help me with this one!' he called. The servants walked up to him. Jeshach, though, did not bend down to help dig out and lift the hefty stone on which Jacob had set his attention. He stood and coughed gently. 'Could I be permitted to volunteer an observation, sir?'

Jacob straightened up and looked, blinking. 'Anything that will help, of course.'

'The dream was given to you, sir. A most remarkable dream, for a most honoured man.' He paused briefly. 'And this is a memorable place indeed, sir. I wonder though, if it would be good, at this juncture, to recall the command within the dream, sir. Could you refresh my memory as to what the voice asked you to do, sir?'

'Yes, um, of course,' said Jacob, not wanting to show too much how bemused he was by the man's sudden loss of short-term memory. 'The voice, God, pointed me to this land, to be my land. This land is my blessing, which will bring blessing to all peoples.'

'A most remarkable promise! At such an opportune time, sir. Bringing blessing to all the families of the earth! It warms the heart, surely.'

'Does that include Hittites?' The younger servant's high

thin voice spoke quietly. The older servant gave him a hard stare and spoke quickly.

'You have indeed been blessed with such a promise, sir. Please do continue. It is such a wonderful message, better and better.'

'Yes, well… Let me see. What came after that? "Know that I am with you and will keep you wherever you go, and will bring you back to this land. I will not leave you until I have done what I have promised you." You see? The land again, this land! We have to mark it. To return to.'

'Thank you, sir. Yes indeed, a tremendous promise of return to this very place. I can see that, sir.' Jacob nodded happily and started to bend over again to the foundation stone for his cairn. 'And the command within the dream, sir! Not only a promise, but a direction. Not only a glorious future, but a guide to your ongoing steps. Not only a future to wait for, but a present reality to engage with. How glorious the vision indeed! And how glorious the instruction, how sweet the command. How blessed are you indeed to have the One and Only guiding you in such an immediate way. Having such a companion, is this not the true blessing?'

Jacob looked at Jeshach bewildered and carried on gathering stones. What was the man on about now?

Miriam suddenly smiled and clapped her hands. She spoke, as though to herself as much as to anyone. 'It's a answer! Where are yer God? What a answer…' She shook her head slowly in wonder.

'The words "Know that I am with you and will keep you," 'Jeshach paused and then stressed the next three words, '… "wherever you go." I think you said that these words were spoken with a little more emphasis, sir? Maybe it would be good to dwell on them at this point?'

Jacob stood back up and looked blank.

'"Wherever you go!"' Caleb cut in again. 'The One is with you in every place. Was the command to know Him here, or everywhere?'

A brief awkward silence. Jacob spoke more slowly. 'The promise, the blessing, they are all tied up with this place, this place is indeed God's house! Come on you two. We'll move, on, of course, but we have to know where to come back to.' He spoke with deliberate emphasis, eyeballing Caleb. 'This is God's House!'

Jeshach and Caleb worked together, Caleb headed to a dip in the ground overlooked by three small shrubs. Jeshach followed more slowly, scouting for stones of medium size, regular enough to form even layers. Sometimes he called Caleb back to help free an embedded stone. They formed little piles to be transported to Jacob's dream site.

Miriam and Hannah started clearing the immediate area, keen that the cairn would have a tidy, distinctive, surround. Jacob stayed with them.

'What has got into those two?' Jacob complained. 'How many other places are as special as this? This must be God's land, God's house.'

'That's a good question.' Hannah dusted down her hands, ready for a longer conversation. Miriam eased herself up too. 'Caleb loves our land too, and he can see even see it greener than this.' She waved her arm over the dry, dusty, wilderness.' He wasn't keen to leave.'

'Do you think I would be travelling unless I had to!' retorted Jacob.

'No, lad,' soothed Miriam. 'You was always so keen to move back to our 'ills.'

'So, it's not that Caleb thinks nothing of this land,' continued Hannah, 'it's that he's focused on what The One has said. That's the way to the blessing, he thinks. Especially the commands. "Securing the blessing our way is disaster. Securing the blessing His way is the heavens on earth." That's one of his sayings.'

'You seem to know a lot about Caleb,' challenged Jacob. 'I didn't know you were so close.'

'I like his passion for The One.' Hannah nodded. 'His words hit home. He makes you think.'

'And he's not bad to look at, with it,' chuckled Miriam. 'Don't yer think that was yer answer, Jakey? O God where are you? Hasn't 'e just said it to yer?'

'Well, he's definitely here at least!' stressed Jacob.

Miriam reached out to rub his arm. 'E said e's with yer Jakey, with yer. E was with your Dad, no doubt about that! E now says e's with you.'

'Like, with you, not above you,' Hannah was hesitant. 'You would have thought the dream meant He was watching from the heavens. On top of the ladder, you know. Sending down the angels. But He said 'Know that I am with you.' Not 'Know that I am above you.' Didn't you think that a bit strange?'

Jacob looked at the young woman. 'Well..., yes..., maybe... When I looked up, and up, I did sort of think I was looking up to The One. The angels were coming from up there, going up there.'

'But the voice you heard didn't come from up there?' Hannah thought aloud. 'That wouldn't have made sense, not with Him saying "Know that I am with you."'

'I thought the voice was coming from next to me. It sounded so close,' pondered Jacob. 'But maybe He can speak from there and the angels helped me to hear it down here?'

'Ooh, I dunno what the two of yer are on about.' Miriam smiled. '"Know that I am wiv yer wherever yer go." That sounds plain and simple to me!'

'Well, He must be up there too, mustn't He?' Hannah's question sounded definite.

'It's too much!' Jacob still sounded cheerful. 'Up, down, there, here, who knows?'

'Caleb might...?' suggested Hannah.

Jacob stamped his right foot on the ground. 'Well, here is where I slept, and here is where I was blessed, and here is where I will return! Here is God's house. He is with me here.'

'Wherever?' suggested Hannah with a smile

'Here!'

'Wherever!'

'Here!"

'You want a marker here, sir; you shall have a marker here, sir.' Hannah walked off to collect more stones.

'Jakey!' Miriam attracted Jacob's attention away from Hannah. 'I think they need some 'elp with them larger stones.'

Jacob headed off to Jeshach and Caleb.

After three armfuls of the major building stones had been carried to site, the team came together for a break

'Congratulations again, sir, on your good morning which has become a good day.' Jeshach beamed. 'Your enthusiasm has led you to the great satisfaction of manual labour.'

'About which you have close knowledge.' cut in Caleb

'Your enthusiasm, sir,' Jeshach ignored the interruption, 'has led you to make full use of your physical prowess. Your stamina is commendable indeed. May I suggest now that you remain here as the master builder, and consider the construction of this pillar-cairn? You will know, sir, the shape and dimensions which will express properly your honourable intentions.'

'Yeah, Jakey' chimed Miriam. 'A break will do yer 'ands good. Yer not so used to this, are yer? I could do with a breather meself.'

The other three loped off to work together. Miriam brushed gravel away from a patch of ground put out a rug. 'Let's 'ave a sit down, Jakey.'

'Aw right?' asked Miriam. 'It's just yer don't seem too comfortable, sort of nervy?'

'Yeah. I'm all right.' Jacob had his head down, playing with the dust between his legs.

'It's a great message, Jakey!' encouraged Miriam. 'Yer blessed, truly blessed. Yer life is going ter be amazing. I think yer more blessed than yer Dad.'

'Yeah.' Jacob turned to his favourite aunt with a faint smile.

'Why yer not more excited? It's like it's made yer afraid.'

'It's pretty overwhelming.' Jacob looked ahead. 'The One can be powerful and fierce and unpredictable. I just want to make sure I pay him proper respect.'

'Relax!' Miriam gave Jacob's arm a playful slap. 'It's all gonna be great! I dunno where yer get the idea The One's nasty. E's going ter bless yer! That's it. Nothin but blessin. Enjoy it!'

'But I could end up in the wrong place,' fretted Jacob,' like Dad could have gone to Egypt. I could upset him in some way and he stops sending the rain.'

'Wrong place?' exclaimed Miriam. 'E's with yer wherever yer go! An if yer mess up, like yer Dad pretendin 'is bootiful wife's 'is sister, 'e'll sort it. Stop yer frettin!

'I wish it were so simple,' groaned Jacob. 'I don't know... I just have a sort of sick feeling inside, like something's not right. Maybe it's because I was short-tempered last night, in such a place as this? I just think I need to be careful.' Jacob shot a little challenging stare at Miriam. 'What's so wrong with that?

'Yer'll be fine Jakey,' soothed Miriam.

When the stone Jacob had put under his head was on top of the pillar, Jacob poured oil on it. It shone in the morning light. 'House of God, Beth El. That's the name for this place now.'

'You know..,' Jacob apologised. The servants understood that he was about to say something which they could not have known. 'I've not been a religious man. I know Grandad

Abraham talked with The One, and Dad always seemed to know the right thing to do. But that was them. I never felt connected to this God. Now I can see myself getting into the worship thing, here. Certainly, if it all does work out.'

"Know that I am with you wherever you go…' muttered Caleb before Jeshach jabbed his back with his staff.

'If The One really will be with me, and really will look after me on this journey I'm on, give me bread to eat and clothes to wear, so that I really do come back to my father's house in peace, then,' Jacob paused briefly, nodding. 'He shall be my God. There. I've said it.' Jacob exhaled with relief and some trepidation.

'Why not now?' whispered the awkward Caleb, this time meriting a heavy jab with the staff on his toe.

'Then this stone, which I have set up for a pillar, shall be God's house. This amazing place will be where I worship. This place of stones, of hidden treasure. This place I would never have wanted to sleep in, let alone live in. This place will be my place.' He exhaled again and blinked. He was surprising himself with his own words.

'And, God! Of all that you give me, I will surely give back to you!' Jacob shouted up to the sky.

'How much?' shot out Caleb. Jeshach grabbed Caleb's cloak to hold him back.

'Yes God!' shouted Jacob. I will give back to you…' Jacob paused, moving his head from side to side, calculating, 'one full tenth!'

'Big promises. Make sure you…' were the last, under the breath, words of the young man, before he was doubled up from a final blow to his chest. Hannah comforted him.

Jacob, oblivious, smiled at his own new-found reverence and generosity, to come. He felt taken up by something unfamiliar, and he felt safer.

'Bravo, sir,' approved Jeshach. 'You have received a wonderful promise of a tremendous blessing to come, a blessing which we look forward to sharing, as we have shared the great blessing on your father. You have exerted yourself to mark this place as a memorial of the promise and the blessing of The One. Such remembrance will entrench and enhance the blessing for you and for many many people. Thank you, sir, for including us in your journey, in your remembrance that The One is with you wherever you go, in your blessing. How blessed we are to walk with the man chosen to be blessed by the One!'

Jacob didn't remember inviting Jeshach to accompany him. He was sure this, too, had been his mother's idea.

Jeshach beamed as he continued. 'We look forward with anticipation to the unfolding and elaboration of the blessing. We know that you are an honorable and upright man who will be careful to adhere to the stipulations of the vow which you have so generously and voluntarily made. The One did not require of you such a commitment and, I am sure, is pleased that you have responded to him in such a definite and measurable, way. I have great confidence, sir, in you remembering and honoring your commitment, as I have the greatest confidence in the One honoring and fulfilling his abundant promises to you, sir. You, and we with you, look forward to a blessed life. Thank you, sir.'

Caleb applauded. Hannah looked at Caleb with a

question on her face. Miriam exclaimed 'O yeah! What a lot we 'ave ter look forward ter!'

Jacob coughed. 'Thank you all for your company. We shall see, shan't we?'

Look forward to

Jacob the Blessed

Love and work and marriage and new families.
Commitment and deception and division.
Nothing is straightforward.
All is blessed.
And then the Wrestling with God.

Jacob the Struggler

Back home and making his own way.
Conflict in the community and the family.
Death and drought.
Joseph has the coloured coat and is torn away.
The final twist: down to Egypt.

Jacob the Full Story

Also by Roger Harper

A British Crash

Death in the city underpass.
By a jilted lover? By a Moslem extremist?
'Easy going, with surprises and sub plots to keep the pages turning.' Sorted Magazine
https://laddermedia.co.uk/a-british-crash-reviews

The Lie of Hell

A fresh look at the old doctrine.
Pastorally helpful, scholarly and accessible
'The fresh perspective… is stimulating and nuanced… likely to invigorate Bible students of all persuasions.' Edward Fudge
Author 'The Fire That Consumes'
Subject of the movie 'Hell and Mr Fudge.'
https://laddermedia.co.uk/lie-of-hell-reviews

Ladder Media Ltd. is a Christian Equitable Company (CEC) – a company where investors and workers love each other as they love themselves.

A CEC is a company limited by guarantee and without a shareholding. Those who invest in the company and those who work for the company are equal partners in running the company and in benefiting from profits.

In a normal shareholding company, the shareholders appoint directors to run the company on their behalf and in their interests. Shareholders take any profit which is not reinvested in the company. Workers receive a salary but normally do not benefit from any increased profit. For workers it has been described as 'working to make other people rich.'

In a normal shareholding company, the shareholders own the company as a piece of property which they can transfer, with continuing entitlement to profit, through generations. This has been the main mechanism through which the gap between the rich and the poor has widened considerably, especially in recent years. Overall, capital is rewarded more than labour. This arrangement is not 'loving your neighbour as you love yourself.'

A cooperative seeks to reverse the inequality, with the workers controlling the company and benefiting from profits. This too is not 'loving your neighbour as you love yourself.'

Christians believe that it is supremely important to love God and to love our neighbour as ourselves in every aspect of our life. Hence the recent formation of the model of a Christian Equitable Company.

Ladder Media Limited is pioneering the development of Christian Equitable companies in the UK.

It is hoped that a Venture Capital CEC, Jerusalem Developments, will soon be formed, to help set up further CECs in the UK and across the world.

For further details or to register an interest in helping with the development of CECs, please write to admin@ laddermedia.co.uk

And did those feet, in ancient time,
Walk upon England's mountains green?
And was the holy lamb of God
In England's pleasant pastures seen?
And did the countenance divine
Shine forth upon our clouded hills?
And was Jerusalem builded here
Among those dark, satanic, mills?

Bring me my bow of burning gold,
Bring me my arrows of desire.
Bring me my spear: O clouds unfold,
Bring me my chariot of fire!
I shall not cease from mental fight,
Nor shall my sword sleep in my hand,
'Til we have built Jerusalem,
In England's green and pleasant land.

William Blake, c1804